I0531071

# 3rd Trip to the Altar

## Superstitious Brides #3

A humorous contemporary romance novella by

# Susan Ann Wall

3RD TRIP TO THE ALTAR

Ebook ISBN: 978-1-941852-16-3
Paperback ISBN: 978-1-941852-17-0

Copyright 2016 Susan Ann Wall, LLC

All Rights Reserved

Cover:
Design: Heart of Jupiter Publishing
Images:  © Shaiith79 | depositphotos.com
         © viknik | depositphotos.com
         © mtruchon | depositphotos.com

Edited by Mary Ann Jock

This is a work of fiction. Names, characters, places, and incidents are a creation from the author's imagination or are used fictitiously.

# Dedication

In memory of Tristin R.
You are still leaving your mark on the world.

~ ♥ ~

Susan Ann Wall

# Chapter 1

"YOU'RE THE GUY, aren't you?" the store clerk asked.

Brent Daniels grunted. He knew what she meant, but maybe if he acted aloof, she'd quit before even getting started.

It had been six days since his dedication aired on that nationally syndicated country radio show. Six days that proved to be pure hell.

"I heard your dedication," the woman continued, all googly-eyed like too many woman had been in the past week. "So romantic. Someone put it to a video on YouTube." She tapped the computer keyboard and the next thing he heard was that country countdown radio show host reading the words Brent had emailed in.

*When I was nineteen, I met a girl who taught me how to love life. She was seventeen and only in town for the summer, but from the moment we met, sparks flew and for three months, we hardly left each other's side. It was the best summer of my life, the best time in my life. I've never found happiness like that again and I often wonder where that wild and crazy girl is who stole my heart and took it with her when she went off to college. It's been ten years, but those memories are as clear and strong as if it was just yesterday. I know I could search her out on social media, but I'm afraid I'll find she's married*

1

*with a couple of kids. I hope she has found happiness, but Tristin May, if you hear this and ever think of me, I'm still here in Lilac Ridge and I'd love to see you again.*

As Eric Church's *Springsteen* faded in, the song yanked at Brent's heart. Every time he heard it, he thought of Tristin, the loneliness burrowing just a little deeper.

"Have you heard from her yet?" the woman asked, eyebrows raised and peering at him as she popped the battery back into his phone.

"No," he growled, through his clenched jaw. Rubbing the back of his neck, Brent hoped this woman, Heather, her name tag read, took the hint that he didn't want to air his dirty laundry. He'd done enough of that on the radio.

"Oh, that's horrible. You poured your heart out and she might not have even heard it."

Brent angled his head to release some of the tension and opened his mouth to crack his jaw, but as the woman kept talking, he continued to grind his teeth. If she didn't finish with his phone soon, he'd have nothing but ash and gums left.

"She's not on Facebook," Heather rambled, batting her eyelashes. "I looked. That's how I recognized you, too. Love your carvings, by the way."

He wasn't so inept with women he didn't recognize this as flirting. He just didn't care. Heather was pretty enough, her sandy brown hair pulled back from her face but falling over her shoulders in waves, eyes bright with hope and anticipation, two things he'd become skilled at destroying with little effort.

With all the date and hate phone calls he'd received, Brent decided it was time to change his number, but it seemed he should have picked a cell phone store where he'd be less recognizable. Maybe one in Tahiti. "Yeah, I, uh, need to get back to work. Can we move this along?"

In truth, he had nowhere to be. He'd checked on the rental units this morning, putting a new padlock on the one where rent hadn't been paid in three months. He had to go back this weekend and empty the thing. The sign business was slow, but the carving business kept him busy as he geared up for summer fairs and craft shows.

"Your phone's all set. Here's the new number." Heather slid a paper across the desk. "I put my number below it, you know, in case she doesn't contact you and you decide to move on."

Brent would put that with the twenty other numbers he'd collected this week, right in the circular file.

He stood to leave, only to meet the scowl of another ex-girlfriend. "You piece of shit," Bailey Hamilton snarled, her hand moving across his face before he could dodge it.

Heather gasped, Bailey smirked, and Brent ignored the burning sting bursting from his cheek.

"Nice to see you too, Bay."

Bailey looked a lot like Heather, pretty, with long brown hair. The difference was the bitterness, in her voice, in her eyes. Brent had put it there.

"Don't give me that. A year, Bear," she groaned, using the nickname he'd been dubbed due to his wood carvings. "I gave you an entire year and it was good. Then you have to pour your heart out on national radio that I wasn't enough, that I didn't make you happy."

It was the same story he'd been hearing all week from most of the women he'd dated over the last ten years. They all took what he'd written out of context. "You did make me happy," he corrected. Just not happy enough.

"That's not what you said on the radio."

Brent threw his arms up in surrender. "Actually, I didn't say anything on the radio. I wrote a letter. It wasn't intended for you or anyone else in Lilac Ridge or a thirty mile radius." Unless Tristin happened to be within that circle, which he doubted. Ten years ago she was just passing through New Hampshire, a summer vacation with her family before she headed for Seattle and the University of Washington. She had loved country music all those years ago, just as Brent did, and listened to the country countdown religiously. He was

3

counting on that to still be part of her routine, but he recognized it for the Hail Mary it was.

Bailey crossed her arms, her chin hitched so high the air had to be thin up there. "Yeah, well we all heard it. We started a group on Facebook."

"Is that so?" he chuckled. These women needed a hobby, a better one than this, anyhow.

"Yes, that is so. We call it *Dissed by Bear Daniels*. There's ten of us."

One woman for every year since he'd spent that summer with Tristin. He didn't want to count them all up, but he was sure there had to be more than ten women he'd dated, and apparently dissed. Some relationships lasted longer than others, but he'd made up for it in between those long terms.

"That's great. I hope it helps all of you. If you'll excuse me."

She side-stepped to block his path. "You don't even care, do you? You don't care how many women you've hurt."

Sighing, he met her angry gaze. "It's been what, two years since we parted ways?"

"One and a half since you dumped me," Bailey corrected.

"We had a good time, Bay, and I'm sorry I hurt you, but I couldn't make you happy for the long haul. We both knew that."

It turned out Brent couldn't make anyone happy for the long haul. It wasn't until Darren's fiancé, Maddie, who had been around that summer when Tristin rattled his cage, did her psychotherapist thing and dug uninvited into his psyche, pointing out the obvious: he couldn't find happiness until he had closure with Tristin.

Bailey huffed, but didn't argue, for which he was grateful.

"See you," he grunted, stepping around her. This time she let him go.

Brent wasn't sure what he hated more, the calls for dates or the confrontations about hurt feelings and broken hearts. He didn't drink anymore, but was ready to throw back a shot of something and put all this behind him.

Six days.

He held little hope of hearing from Tristin at this point. She wasn't on Facebook, as Heather had pointed out, at least not as Tristin May. Brent's sister had looked after she, too heard the dedication. There were three radio stations to tune into in Lilac Ridge. Seemed the country station was the most popular based on the response he'd received.

Despite not being a betting man, he put a Benjamin down his theory being spot on. Tristin was happily married with a few kids. He doubted she was even the same wild and carefree girl he'd known all those years ago. Lord knew he had grown out of his rebellious ways, out of necessity, not choice, but the only regrets he had were the circumstances that forced him to change, not the change itself.

Brent's truck auto-piloted to the opposite side of town. His sister's old Beetle was parked in Madigan's dirt lot. Since she was better known for being late than early, he guessed Courtney took an early break from fielding desperate and angry phone calls on his behalf. It was a small price to pay for the job he'd given her, a job he could have hired someone else to do for minimum wage. Courtney scheduled appointments, took orders, handled his email, website, and Facebook page, and answered the phones. Okay, so maybe no one would do all that for minimum wage. He'd pay her more if he could afford to, but this job gave his sister the flexibility she needed to go to college and volunteer at the animal rescue.

Plus, there was that time she made him feed a couple king snakes at the rescue. No amount of phone calls could ever recoup the psychological trauma of that event.

He was only a few steps into the pub when that damned dedication wafted from the speakers.

Brent scowled at Sean Beckett, who stood behind the bar with a shit-eating grin on his scruffy mug. Brent flipped him the bird as he crossed the room to where Courtney sat at a booth.

"Hey, sis," he said, sliding in opposite her.

Courtney's spunky brown waves were pulled into a loose pony tail, rogue strands falling around her long face. "I quit," she declared, looking up from the tablet.

"How many calls since I left?" He was almost afraid to ask, but conversation needed to start somewhere.

"Death threats or dates?" Courtney chuffed.

"Aren't they one in the same?" he responded.

"You even have women tagging you in half naked pictures, claiming you're not all that." She turned the tablet to show him one of the pictures.

Brent kept fit by wielding a chainsaw and other power tools as part of his craft, and hauling other people's junk out of the storage units they refused to pay rent on. He was a meat and potatoes kind of man, but since he'd quit drinking years ago, he had stopped carrying around unnecessary baggage. "I'm not all that," he shrugged.

"I know," Courtney said. He could always count on his baby sister to massage his delicate ego.

"What are you working on?" he asked as she continued to tap away on the tablet.

"Damage control," she groaned. "I don't get paid for damage control."

"Lunch is on me," he offered.

Courtney stopped tapping and looked at him, her left eyebrow raised. "Lunch is always on you." After an eye-roll and a shake of her head, she went back to the tablet.

With half-naked pictures claiming he wasn't all that floating around Facebook, Brent didn't want to imagine what "damage control" might entail, but he was grateful Courtney had his back.

"Maybe I need to get on one of those dating sites," he said, resigning to his fate. Tristin was in the wind and the weather didn't seem to want to send her his way. It'd been a long time, damn long. That stupid radio dedication did nothing for his cause except create drama and headaches. It was time to let go, give someone a chance at making him happy, and him making her happy in return.

"You're kidding right? I've been after you for months to do that, but no, you have to pour your heart out on the radio instead. You don't have a chance of finding someone true now."

Brent would bang his head against the table if he was the bang-his-head-against-the-table kind of guy. He wasn't. He'd always been a man of action, always. He proved that today by changing his number.

"I'm sorry," he offered, only because he was sorry for the trouble he'd caused his sister. He wasn't sorry for trying to reach out to Tristin. He gave it the old college try. Now he needed to move on. Officially.

"Just, ugh, you are infuriating!"

"It could be worse," he said.

Courtney's head bobbed back and forth as she contemplated that. "You're right. Thank you for not drinking."

"I love you, Court. I don't mean to make life difficult for you."

After a long sigh, she shook her head at him. "You're not. I'm glad you tried. Sorry it didn't work out."

Brent shrugged, though the disappointment rushing through him was far from the indifference that had been drilled into the Daniels' kids. "Does it make me a wus to want to settle down, find love, have a couple kids?"

"Makes you human," she said, "but you might not want to admit that to too many people if you want to keep your bad-ass Bear Daniels reputation."

Brent didn't give a shit about his reputation.

"You got your eye on anyone?" he asked, almost afraid of the answer. He loved his sister, but her biggest fault was the stubborn independence she lived by. He just wanted to see her happy.

"Between school, work, and the rescue, I don't even have time for my vibrator."

"Court," he groaned. "That's gross."

"Only because I'm your sister. Any other chick and it'd be hot, so on top of everything else, I also have to live under your umbrella of double standards."

Brent would never admit to that, but she'd hit the mark on the first try.

Sean came up to the table, pen behind his ear, dish towel thrown over his shoulder. "Sorry to keep you waiting. I'm all alone today."

"No worries," Brent offered. He liked hanging out with his sister, even if the conversation did straddle the line of appropriate.

"I'll have the grilled chicken salad, vinaigrette on the side and a Diet Coke with a wedge — not a slice — of lemon." Courtney always ordered rabbit food and a stupid wedge in that bitter aftertaste soda. She was this tiny little thing who could stand to gain some weight on her bones. He wished she'd eat a steak and fries and go for the full calorie drink.

"Got it," Sean said, the pen still behind his ear as he turned to Brent.

"Bohemian Burger," Brent said, not even bothering to look at the menu. "Medium rare with cole-slaw and a Coke, not diet, no lemon, wedge or otherwise."

Sean snickered and nodded. "Thanks guys. It won't be long. At least the kitchen staff is all here today."

Brent turned from Sean to find Courtney staring at him.

"What?" he asked.

"You're a man seeking a woman, I assume?"

He had no idea where this question had come from. "I think that's obvious."

"What age? 25 is too young for you, but we don't want to rule out child-bearing years. Let's go with 28 to 33."

"Court, what are you doing?"

"Dating site. You said you were ready. I'm getting you started." She tapped on the tablet until their food arrived, ignoring all his reluctant yet curious inquiries.

8

He'd regret this, of that he had no doubt, but he also knew how to pick his battles. Court would do this with or without his blessing. She was the type of person who took a mile when offered an inch. Given that he'd been forced to abandon her when she was still just a kid and he'd been her only ally in the Daniels' house, he owed it to her to let this play out.

"Holy shit, that's a lot of information for *free* browsing," she sighed, using air quotes when she said the word *free*.

"What exactly does that mean?" he asked.

She didn't answer, just slid the tablet across the table and picked up her fork. "I'd kill for pasta," she whined.

"Then why didn't you order pasta?" he asked, ignoring the tablet.

"Pasta is empty calories and I don't have time to work off empty calories."

Brent shook his head, taking a bite of the loaded burger and acknowledging internally that he'd never understand women, not even the ones he shared DNA with. As he chewed, the tablet's screen went black, relief pouring through him. He had no interest in being on a dating site, no interest in dating. Not unless it involved a certain woman who had been just a girl when she'd wrecked him for all other women.

# Chapter 2

"THIS IS THE cutest town I've ever seen," Cyn cooed as she hobbled across the dirt parking lot. The crutches were too small, but at least she was using them, a feat in itself.

"It hasn't changed at all," Tristin said, pulling off her helmet and letting mountain air fill her lungs. She moved too often for any place except the RV to feel like home, but as she stretched her legs after the long ride, she felt like she'd just tapped her leather boots together and whispered, *"There's no place like home."*

"I can't believe you'd choose food over seeing your hunka hunka." Cynthia Munn was Tristin's partner in crime, and despite Tristin's objections about this little trip down memory lane, Cyn waved her magic wand and made it all happen.

It had been a long ride to New Hampshire, several states off target of their original destination, and a ride Tristin wasn't seasoned for. "I've never ridden the bike that long. I'm famished." Plus, she needed a shower to wash the miles off and to freshen up before seeing Brent for the first time in ten years.

And maybe she was stalling, just a little.

Putting the helmet on the seat of the Harley, Tristin squatted and stretched, squatted and stretched, and what the hell, did it one more time for good measure, pushing the last 200 miles of stiffness out of her body. "How's the leg?"

Cyn grunted. "I can't believe I have to spend the summer in a cast. I hope that guy never ends up on my surgical table."

Eight days ago, Tristin and Cyn headed out from New Orleans, en route to Wisconsin for a summer of fun. After two days in Memphis, they were at the campground gift store getting ready to get back on the road when they heard that dedication on the radio. Cyn canceled their Wisconsin reservations and booked them at the Lilac Ridge Family Campground for the summer before Tristin could voice any objections. What should have been a two-day trek turned into disaster when some jackass cut Cyn off and sent her Jeep and the trailer she pulled skidding off the road and tumbling down an embankment. She was lucky to only have broken her foot, but Tristin knew she'd milk it as if plastered into a full-body cast.

It also changed their travel plans. With the Jeep still in a body shop in Hartford, they needed to offload the Harley from the truck to make room for the contents of the trailer. Cyn drove the truck that pulled their RV and Tristin rode the bike for the last leg. They'd go back next week to pick up the Jeep and the trailer.

"Let's get some lunch," Tristin said when her stomach rumbled. She'd loved Madigan's Pub and had been lucky enough that summer when she was seventeen to have a fake ID to enjoy all the microbrews on tap. She wondered if they still brewed their own beers.

Tristin trudged into the pub, so desperate for something, anything, she didn't much care if the food was still good. If tripe was the only thing on the menu, she'd devour it without a second thought.

"I'm having a margarita," Cyn declared. "I don't care what the warning label says on those pain killers."

Tristin made a note to bribe the server into bringing a margarita of the virgin variety, otherwise, the scene could turn ugly fast. "Do whatcha gotta do," she sang, walking toward the pub door.

Brent was the one to get her the fake ID, at the same time he got his own. The first thing they'd done was buy a twelve pack at the convenience store and hit the lake. Then they'd gotten matching tattoos.

The infinity symbol was Tristin's first tattoo, but Brent's shoulder and chest were already covered in ink. He had looked much older than nineteen, broad shoulders and facial hair masking the youth beneath. Based on the pictures Cyn insisted on showing her from Facebook, he'd gotten even broader, his sex appeal going from bad-boy yum to solid hunk of sexy man.

Of course, Tristin hadn't missed the captions with the photos. Women he'd dated weren't happy about the radio dedication, feeling jilted by his heartfelt message. Tristin laughed it off. Women could be so dramatic. Present company included.

Mixed feelings about the dedication flitted around in her head and heart. It was sweet, stirring feelings she'd pushed aside and ignored for years. On the opposite end of the spectrum, it was like walking into a dark, dank cellar, inspiring a ridiculous fear she couldn't control. What if she didn't live up to Brent's expectations, or worse, what if she did? This pit stop in Lilac Ridge was just that, temporary. In September she'd be on her way to Wyoming and who knows where after that, though she had her sites set on San Diego.

After pulling the door open, she let Cyn hobble through first, but even with a broken foot, her friend had the fortitude to hold the second door for Tristin. When she walked into the dimly lit pub, her steps came to a halt in front of a bear of a man.

Her gaze lifted and breath lodged somewhere in her respiratory system when she met the dark eyes of the man who'd enticed her to return to Lilac Ridge.

"Tristin." Her name was a mere whisper on Brent's lips, but held enough power to dissolve the hell of the last four days and set the entire building on fire.

*If I whispered your name I bet there'd still be a spark.*

Then and there Tristin acknowledged the truth of the words to that Eric Church song, the song Brent had so aptly dedicated to her.

"Hi," she breathed, heart tumbling into her stomach. All the blood rushed from her head, leaving her dizzy and stupid. "I heard your dedication."

Brent stood there, staring, probably because it was the stupidest thing she could have said. Of course she'd heard it, why else would she be here?

As he continued to stare and shake his head, Tristin hoped it was shock at seeing her, not disappointment. She hadn't dressed for the occasion, not expecting to run into him in this pub after she'd spent the last four hours on the road. Wearing cargo pants because her only other options were cut-offs or a little red dress she never had the occasion to wear, Tristin realized she had to work on the wardrobe situation. Nothing said *I'm Not Sexy* like cargo pants. Well, except nurse's scrubs.

"Yeah, I, uh," he stumbled before shaking his head. "Dammit, woman, you're so beautiful I don't even know what to say,"

Beautiful…when was the last time a man had uttered that word in praise to her? Never, well, no one other than… "Brent," she whispered, a rare blush burning her cheeks.

"Ohmigod, she calls you Brent," the woman next to him giggled.

Shaking herself out of the dazed and aroused state, Tristin looked at the woman, who somehow seemed familiar. "What else would I call him?"

13

"Most people call me Bear, because of the carvings, and…"

When she looked back at him, the words trailed off, his piercing gaze making every nerve ending in her body aware of the attention.

"Everyone calls him Bear," the curly haired woman interjected. "Except me. He's more of a pussy cat than a bear anyway."

"Court," Brent groaned.

"What? You are."

"Well, Pussy Cat," Cyn purred from over Tristin's shoulder, "I convinced her to come, so I expect the first child to be named after me."

"Cyn," Tristin groaned now.

"Sorry, I have first dibs on first born's name," the other woman declared. "I've been fielding phone calls from love struck women who want to date him and angry ex-girlfriends who want to strangle him."

"And you are?" Cyn inquired, ever the protective one, but Tristin was curious too.

"Courtney, the sister," she sang, extending her arm.

Cyn grabbed it. "Cyn, the best friend, roommate, partner in crime…master navigator."

Captain Crash would be a better descriptor, but since Cyn nursed a broken foot from the accident, Tristin opted to keep that nickname to herself. With her gaze still fixed on Brent, Tristin suggest, "maybe we should leave and let these two get better acquainted."

"I'm almost as afraid to leave them unsupervised as I am to stay here," he said. She'd expected him to take her hand or put an arm around her, but he just stood there, looking as surprised as she felt. "I can't believe you're here."

When Tristin wove her arm around his because she couldn't spend another second not touching him, fire and rainbows rushed through her.

Yeah, there was still a spark.

14

"I can't believe it either," she said, shocked by the energy surging between them. It had been just as powerful when she was seventeen and they met at the lake where all the teens hung out.

Tristin had been worried about two things. First, she worried there wouldn't be a spark after all this time. That worry was extinguished in an instant, pouring gasoline on the other worry, that there would be a spark. Her time in Lilac Ridge was short, again, just a summer. Based on the radio show dedication, Brent wanted more than a summer fling, but a summer together was all she could offer.

"Where do you want to go?" he asked.

Tristin nodded. "I'm starving. I know you were just leaving, but I'm borderline hangry."

His smile took the sparks passing between them and made them jump and sizzle.

"Ohmigod," his sister cooed. "He never smiles. Nev-er!"

Tristin remembered Brent always being serious, almost somber, when they were in a group, but never when they were alone. His smile, mischievous and filled with sultry promises, had been one of the things she loved about him all those years ago.

"Come on," he said. "Let's get you some food and tame that hangry beast before it unleashes on Tweety-Bird over here."

"Do not call me that in public," Courtney demanded. "Or ever. Don't ever call me that."

Walking with Brent, he claimed a booth in the back of the quiet pub. "What's good here?" she asked, grabbing a menu from the plastic tray at the end of the table.

"Everything," he murmured. "Though I can't speak personally for the salads, but Court seems to enjoy them."

Tristin raised a brow. "Do you really think a salad is going to tame the hangry beast in me?"

Brent shrugged, his smile fading. "I have no idea. Women always seem to go for salads and you're a woman."

15

The server came over, a tall, well-built guy with a friendly smile and trimmed brown hair. "Eating again, man?" he asked.

"Just a Coke for me and whatever the lady wants."

"The Bohemian Burger with fries — loaded, please."

Both men snickered. "What?" she asked.

"You'll like it," Brent offered. "It's what I always get."

Tristin noticed Cyn and Courtney take a seat at the bar, both of them angled to watch Tristin and Brent, as if they were some sort of freak show. "Oh, and please don't let my friend charm you into serving her any alcohol. She's on prescription painkillers and shouldn't be mixing it."

"Gotcha," the guy said, clicking his tongue and winking.

"I'm not kidding," Tristin declared in opposition to his casual response. She pointed a finger at him. "I will hold you personally responsible for anything that happens to her if you serve her alcohol."

"Sean's good," Brent assured her. "Sean Beckett, meet Tristin May."

The guy's eyes widened to the size of bowling balls. "The girl from the radio."

"I'm not actually *from* the radio," she corrected.

"Right, well, wow, it's nice to meet you."

She shook hands with him. "I was in the army the summer you were here, but I'm a native. Try not to hold that against me."

"I'll take it under advisement," she laughed. "Nice to meet you, but seriously, you serve Cyn alcohol and I will torture you. Since I'm a nurse, I knew how to do it to maximize the pain without leaving a mark."

"Noted," he said, winking once more before retreating to the bar.

"You're still tough," Brent smiled.

"Gotta be," she shrugged before nodding in the direction of the bar. "We have an audience."

Brent gave a quick glance over his shoulder, rolling his eyes as he focused on Tristin, taking her hands in his.

"I can ignore them if you can," he said.

While Cyn was Tristin's best friend — and yes, partner in crime — she had learned to ignore the less charming behavior, particularly the incessant matchmaking. Tristin didn't believe in happily ever afters the way Cyn did. "I can ignore them."

Silence extended as they just looked at each other. It should be uncomfortable, but not only could Tristin not look away, she couldn't bring herself to ruin the refamiliarization brewing between them. His rough hands warmed her as his thumb moved back and forth over hers, making her a little shaky and a lot hot.

"That dedication was a shot in the dark," he sighed, pulling one hand across the table and pressing his lips to it.

"I was in a gift shop in Tennessee," she replied. The dedication had stopped her in her tracks. Her heart had yet to recover.

"Tennessee? Is that where you live?"

Tristin shook her head. "No, I don't live anywhere, at least not for long. Three to six months, max, depending on the contract. I hate the long ones."

"Contract?"

"Cyn and I are traveling nurses. We go where the work is, but we take the summers off to live a little. We just finished a gig in Texas and were on our way to Wisconsin when we heard the dedication."

"Wisconsin," he sighed, the same disappointment reflected on his face.

"We've never been to Wisconsin. We always go someplace we haven't been before."

"Is it just the two of you?" he asked. She knew what he alluded to and decided to toss him a life jacket.

Tristin smile and squeezed his hand. "Yeah, me and Cyn. We travel together. I don't have a boyfriend," she assured him. "And, we're here for the summer. No Wisconsin."

"The summer?" he smiled, the excitement returning to his eyes.

Tristin smiled too. "The whole summer. We have to leave the first week of September to make it to Wyoming in time for our next job."

He seemed interested, but Tristin's skeptical side prickled. This all seemed too good to be true and she'd learned the hard way that if it seemed too good, she'd better brace for the fall.

"I thought maybe you'd be married with a couple kids and a big house with a white picket fence out front," Brent said.

She laughed because if she'd gone through with her first wedding, she might be stuck in that kind of life, the kind she wasn't at all interested in. "No husband. No kids. No fence."

His smile lifted all the way to his eyes, the relief relaxing the tight grip he had on her hands.

A noisy group of women entered the pub. Brent turned, groaning as he turned back to Tristin. "I'm so sorry for what's about to happen."

One of the women spotted them and came marching to the table, anger seething from every pore.

"Oh, honey, you must be new in town," her shrill voice uttered.

"Something like that," Tristin replied, putting her focus on Brent and smiling.

"Well, I feel compelled to warn you about Bear here," she said, her voice now rumbling with a growl as if she was channeling her own inner bear.

Tristin didn't hide her annoyance at the unwanted interruption but leaned back in the booth to have a better angle at sizing this woman up. "Warn me?"

"He's nice to look at, there's no denying that, but he's emotionally unavailable. It may not seem that way at first, but trust me, trust all of us," she said waving her hand at the group of women who gawked from the middle of the pub. "He's pining after this woman who most of us believe doesn't even exist."

"Really?" Tristin asked, intrigued. She smiled and winked at Brent before giving her attention back to the woman.

"Yes, really. All of us, who have been stretched through the wringer, we started a pool."

"What kind of pool?" Tristin asked through Brent's groan.

"We call it the *Woman Who Doesn't Exist Pool*. It's a twenty-five dollar buy-in and you have to pick a date when you think Bear will admit this woman isn't real."

"That's interesting," Tristin said. "But I'm confused, what makes you think he's pining after a woman who doesn't exist?"

The woman's dramatic gasp had Tristin biting her tongue to keep from laughing. "You don't know about the radio dedication?"

Tristin smirked at Brent for a second. "Tell me about it."

"Well, he dedicated this song on national radio, pouring his heart out about how she showed him the best summer of his life and that he's never found that kind of happiness since."

"Sounds romantic," Tristin cooed.

"Oh, honey, don't let him fool you. It's pathetic."

"What's the pot on the pool?"

"We're up to $500."

"And what if I believe the woman does exist?"

"You can buy in on that too, but that's a fool's bet. You have to produce proof to win the pot."

"Sounds fair," Tristin said and dug into her pocket. Slapping thirty dollars on the table, she asked, "Can you make change?"

"Of course." The women reached into her large purse and pulled out an envelope, sliding a five dollar bill from it. She grabbed Tristin's money and slid it into the envelope. Then she tapped on her phone. "I keep the list here. What's your name, honey?"

"TM," Tristin offered.

"TM?" the woman questioned.

"Yeah, that's what some of my friends call me. It's the whole Harley thing." It was total BS, but this woman was too easy to toy with.

19

"I don't follow," the woman said.

Tristin shrugged. "It's not important. What kind of proof are you looking for?"

"It has to be a picture, of one Tristin May here in Lilac Ridge or one with her and Bear." Tristin had pictures of her and Bear stashed away in her Pandora's box, but she didn't want to share those with this bitter woman.

"You know what she looks like?" Tristin asked.

"No, but a few claim to know her. They put in their wagers and said they'd dig up proof, but so far, they've come up empty."

"Really, who thinks she exists?"

"Maddie Carson and Clarissa Dean, for starters. Those two are thick as thieves, watch out for them. Cat Merriweather, too. They claim to have met her that summer, but I think they're just sticking up for Bear."

Tristin smiled. She remembered all three of them was happy to hear they were still here. She a mental note to reconnect with them. "What about Matt Carson? Did he place a wager?" she asked.

"Oh, no, he's away in the army. Wait, how do you know Matt?"

Tristin shrugged and reached into her purse. "I assume legal ID is valid proof?"

Brent chuckled now and shook his head.

"What? Legal ID? What did you say your name is?"

"TM. Those are my initials," Tristin said, handing her driver's license to the queen of bitter.

The queen let out another dramatic gasp. "You're Tristin May?" she said before the shock morphed into anger. "You swindled me."

"You were willing to take my twenty-five dollar buy-in. Maybe you need to find some other way to work out your issues with Brent. I'll take my winnings," Tristin said, holding out her hand.

The woman huffed and slapped the envelope into Tristin's

hand.

"As for Brent being emotionally unavailable, I'm willing to find that out on my own, not from a bunch of Stepford wife wannabes. Have a nice day." Tristin would bet the entire pool she'd just won that Brent was more available in that department than she was, but since she was only here for the summer, there was no need to explore any lingering or long-term issues.

The woman just stood there, shooting daggers at Tristin.

"I'm sorry, maybe I wasn't clear," Tristin stated, the warning now deliberate and clear in her voice. "That was your cue to leave. Bye-bye now."

"Well, I never," the woman huffed.

"I'm sure that's true," Tristin laughed, counting the cash as the woman huffed once more and stomped off. When she left the bar, the rest of the women followed.

Brent laughed, all the tension gone.

As Sean stepped up to the table with her burger, Cyn and Courtney rushed across the bar, Cyn holding up her hand. Tristin slapped her the high-five.

"Did you just hustle Bailey Hamilton out of the *Woman Who Doesn't Exist* pool?" Courtney asked, wide-eyed. "And then call her a Stepford wife?"

"I won the pool fair and square," Tristin said, tucking the money away and biting into her burger, which — OH EM GEE — was heaven wrapped in toasted bread.

Brent's eyes widened as she groaned and she didn't miss the tell-tale shift in his seat.

Good Goddess, the man was gorgeous and sexy and being with him for just these few minutes, it didn't seem like a decade had passed. Tristin would never wish to be a teenager again, but he stirred things in her, the longing, the need, the heat. He was dangerous, but she'd always loved living on the edge. Three months wasn't going to be long enough, but she would make the most of every second she had here in Lilac Ridge.

21

"I thought for sure I'd win that pool. I know he has pictures of you stashed somewhere, but do you think he'd let me have one, just to knock Bailey off her marble pedestal? No."

"I was waiting for the pool to hit $1000. That would have been a big score for you," Brent defended.

Bailey dug into the envelope and pulled out $25. "Here. Consider yourself reimbursed. I only want to take money from the vengeful, not the believers."

"You are so cool," Courtney said, tucking the money in her pocket.

"I second that," Brent added. "No one sends Bailey away with her tail tucked between her legs. I'd pay to see that again."

Tristin laughed. "Well, Bailey Hamilton and her friends just paid for a month of campground fees."

"Right," Cyn drawled, "about that. I found us a better deal. Courtney offered us space at her house. There's water and electric hookup, we'd just have to use the dump tank."

"What?" Tristin asked, stunned. She looked at Courtney. "Where do you live?"

"She lives with me," Brent cut in. "She's offering a spot on my land."

# Chapter 3

THERE WAS A time when Tristin reacted on impulse, not worried about the consequences. Her parents would argue she still lived that way, but she liked to classify herself as a responsible adult.

Most of the time.

Ten years ago ... hell, even six years ago, she would have jumped at the opportunity to park the RV for free for the summer. Not only would they save $1500 in campground fees, but she could pocket the $500 she'd just scored.

"We don't want to impose," Tristin said. She didn't want to invade Brent's space, but she also didn't want him invading hers. While Brent had never been controlling that summer she'd spent in Lilac Ridge, they'd both grown-up since then and she valued her independence above everything else. Two too many times she had given her heart and lost a piece of herself. Since she was only her for the summer, she needed to keep some reasonable distance between them, not just so she didn't get lost, but so she didn't hurt Brent in the process.

Brent had been safe all those years ago and she'd suffered nothing but a broken heart when she had to leave for college. Ten years had passed, though. That was almost a lifetime. For some of her patients, it had been. Tristin had changed, and she'd bet the pot Brent had too.

Sitting across the booth while she waited for lunch was easy, just like it had been that summer they met and fell in love. Living on the same property, that would create expectations she wasn't sure she could live up to.

"You're not imposing. You have an RV?" Brent asked.

"Yeah, like I said, home is wherever I park my truck." Because her truck pulled the RV.

"The spot Court referred to is private. You can't see the house. I parked my own RV there while building the cabin."

"You built a cabin?" Tristin asked. Why didn't this surprise her?

Brent nodded. "Yeah, someplace to call my own. My shop is there too. I make signs and do wood carvings. That's why people call me Bear. Bears are my specialty."

"That is so cool," Tristin said. "I really don't want to impose." Saving money, though, that was something she couldn't resist. She was building a nest egg for when the day came that she did want to plant some roots. She lived by a strict budget, with a financial plan that included savings, investments, money for living expenses, and a little bit to have some fun.

"You aren't," he insisted.

"Can we at least pay for water and electric? Cyn takes long showers."

"True story," Cyn said.

"We can talk about it," Brent said. "But you're here because of me, so offering a place to stay is the least I can do."

"I already canceled the campground," Cyn said, raising her brow to dare Tristin to challenge how she handled the logistics of their lifestyle.

It seemed Cyn had taken it upon herself to handle the

logistics of Tristin's love life too. While Tristin was ready to strangle her friend for the campground cancellations, all she could do was smile. If Cyn didn't take care of all that garbage, Tristin would have to. She'd rather handle the logistics once they arrived than deal with reservations and contracts.

"It's settled then," Brent said. "When you're done eating, you can follow me. We're a few miles out of town. It's quiet."

Cyn and Courtney did a little happy dance, as if they'd been friends their whole lives. When the joyful celebration ended, the two joined them — uninvited — and while Tristin finished her burger and Cyn gobbled up a salad, Courtney talked about the animal rescue where she volunteered, trying to convince everyone at the table, Brent included, to adopt a pet.

The RV was barely big enough for the two of them, never mind a furry friend. Plus, when they worked, their days were long, and when they didn't work, they liked to play. It wasn't a lifestyle that invited the responsibility of a pet.

When the food was gone and the bill paid — courtesy of the pool winnings, they headed out of the pub, Brent placing a possessive hand on the small of Tristin's back that sent a zinger of awareness. To every. Last. Nerve.

By the time they reached her truck and motorcycle, she was out of breath, the short walk having nothing to do with it.

"You weren't kidding about the Harley thing," Brent said. "She's a beauty."

"He," Tristin corrected. "You don't really think I'd straddle a 'she' for the long haul, do you?"

Brent laughed. "Well, a man can fantasize."

"Typical," Cyn and Courtney muttered in perfect harmony.

"He's got some power," Tristin said, focusing on the bike and not Brent's wayward fantasies. "It's not a little girl's bike." Tristin was small, as she'd been reminded her whole life, but that didn't mean she couldn't wield the power of a Harley Davidson. The Sportster SuperLow was the perfect ride, but Tristin wasn't used to long rides like she'd endured the last two days. She was ready to sleep for a week.

"I wouldn't expect you to ride a little girl's bike," Brent said.

"You still ride?" she asked, hopeful he did. Her interest in motorcycles sparked long before she met Brent, but it was his encouragement that put her on the path to getting her own bike instead of riding bitch all the time.

"Yeah. I've got a Harley Fat Bob. She," he emphasized, "has a lot of power."

"We'll have to go for a ride," Tristin suggested, willing to give up the reigns for a ride on the back of Brent's bike. She'd always liked that intimacy, her thighs pressed against his, arms clung around his waist. He didn't have a Harley back then, but Tristin was too young and horny to care about what kind of bike he had. The fact he had one at all hooked her line and sinker.

"I have a boat now too. We can go out on the lake without borrowing."

By borrowing he meant stealing, even though they did return the stolen boat before they got caught. Lots of rich people lived on Starlight Lake and because it was a small town, they lived under the blanket of safety only found in a small town. The only real threat was teenagers looking for a good time.

"Sounds fun. I still suck at fishing."

"I seem to recall you were pretty good at it."

Tristin's idea of fishing was putting the line in the water and letting the pole dangle over her leg while she and Brent made out like manic teenagers until there was a tug on the line. Even then, if things had progressed far enough, she'd just toss the pole aside for a more enticing rod.

Not one to blush, the fact her cheeks burned embarrassed Tristin even more.

"Pretty," he said, brushing her cheek with his knuckles and stirring that awareness even more.

"Charmer," she murmured, nuzzling his hand for a brief

moment. "So I guess we're following you?" she asked Brent, abandoning his affectionate touch to grab her jacket and helmet.

Brent nodded and headed across the dirt parking lot to a black truck that looked a lot like Tristin's. She climbed on the Harley, fired it up, and let Cyn fall in with the truck behind Brent. Cyn's Jeep was still in Connecticut. They decided they'd get settled in Lilac Ridge and go back for the trailer when the body work on the Jeep was complete. They'd loaded most of the contents of the trailer into Tristin's truck, which had plenty of room once they took the Harley out. Cyn could manage the truck with a broken leg since it was an automatic, and even though it had kicked her ass, Tristin enjoyed the long ride on the Harley.

With Courtney bringing up the rear in their little caravan, they rolled through town, turning onto a secondary road after a few miles. About a mile onto that road, they turned down a dirt road, but Tristin soon realized it was a driveway. Moving slowly after a few hundred yards, the convoy came to a stop. If this is where they were parking the RV, Tristin would have to take over the wheel because Cyn couldn't back the thing in to save her life.

After setting the helmet on the bike, she strode down, meeting Brent next to her truck. "Twenty-five yards down this path is the lot for the camper. There's plenty of room to turn around and back it in. It might be easiest if I bring it down."

"I can handle it," Tristin said, not one to accept help — ever. "You can ride shotgun and be my navigator," she offered.

He chuckled and nodded, a sexy smile curving his mouth as he sauntered around the truck.

"He is so hot for you," Cyn whispered as she climbed down.

"Shush," Tristin said, giving Cyn a shoulder shove as the two passed.

"Classy," Cyn drawled. "Good thing I'm forgiving."

27

"Good thing I am, too," Tristin added, climbing into the truck.

"How long you been doing this?" Brent asked when she started down the path in low gear.

"Living out of an RV or doing the traveling nurse thing?" she asked.

"Both."

"I've been doing the traveling nurse thing with Cyn for about five years. She's been doing it longer. The job offers a housing allowance, but by rooming together, we were able to put half of that away to save up for the RV. We bought this three years ago. Cyn's backed it into two trees and almost took out my Harley once. I haven't let her back it up since."

"You two are pretty tight, huh?"

"Yeah. She's like the sister I always wanted," Tristin said.

He chuckled. Like Brent, Tristin had a younger sibling. Unlike Brent and his sister, Tristin and Troy, who was perfect in every way, weren't all that close. "How are your folks? Your dad still serving?"

"Nope, retired after I graduated college. They bought a place in San Antonio and my dad works as a consultant at Randolph Air Force Base. Mom, of course, is still doing the nursing thing at one of the military hospitals. Troy followed in Dad's footsteps."

"Do they know you're here?" he asked. Her parents didn't approve of Brent back when she was seventeen, which only made him more enticing back then.

"Worried they might ground me to keep me from seeing you?"

He chuckled. "I'd hope we've outgrown that."

"They know I'm here. They don't know why." Tristin didn't feel compelled to share the radio dedication with them, but when her mother asked if she planned to see that boy who had ruined her as a young girl, Tristin was happy to torment her mother with a yes.

Brent grunted, and she wasn't sure how to take that so she

turned the conversation to him. "How about your Uncle Ray?"

"He died a few years ago. Heart attack."

"Oh, Brent, I'm so sorry." Ray had taken Brent in when his parents kicked him out. Tristin had met him a couple times and while he was a little rough around the edges, always with a beer and a cigarette, he wasn't horrible.

"Thanks. The smoking and drinking caught up with him."

"And your parents?" she asked.

"Same. In the wind. Courtney hears from them on occasion, but we haven't seen them."

"You okay with that?" she asked. Brent had felt abandoned when his parents sent him to Lilac Ridge to live with his mother's brother. Both parents were alcoholics and neither of them could hold a job, so they moved often, even more often than Tristin had growing up as an air force brat.

"I am. Court's still pretty bitter. She served in the air force for six years. She's living with me while she goes to college."

"She's feisty," Tristin laughed.

"You have no idea. There's the spot there." The path opened to a small clearing with plenty of room to maneuver the RV in.

With precision, she backed the RV into the spot, finding Brent smiling at her when she cut the engine. Cyn and Courtney walked down the path, chatting as if they'd been friends forever. Cyn's dad died when she was young and her mother ditched her with her paternal grandmother. Cyn claimed not to have abandonment issues, but Tristin saw it at times. It was no surprise she'd bond immediately with someone who had a situation similar to hers.

"This is sweet," Cyn cooed as they stopped at the back of the truck where Tristin and Brent went to work unhitching the RV. Cyn grabbed the tire blocks, handing one to Courtney, and the both moved to the back of the RV to secure the tires.

Tristin didn't have to give Brent any direction. He took the initiative — and the lead — using that male strength to release the chains and latch. She could have left him to it, but this was her responsibility, so Tristin did her part. They fell into an easy rhythm, getting the trailer unhooked from the truck and then getting the water and electric lines connected.

"I have to turn the valve on and hit the breaker on my end, but other than that, you should be all set."

"Thanks. We appreciate this."

Brent stepped up to her, his hand cupping her jaw as his thumb caressed her cheek. It was like he'd hit that breaker and the electric line was hooked up to her instead of the camper.

"I appreciate you being here."

Tristin licked her lips, drawing his gaze there for a moment. He leaned in and she went on up on her toes because flat-footed she only came up to his shoulders.

When she thought he'd press his lips to hers, he sighed. "I'd kiss you, but we have an audience," he whispered.

"I don't care," Tristin said, both hands moving to cup his nape to pull him down to her. When their lips met, that electric charge surged.

~♥~

Tristin had never been shy, something he'd loved about her all those years ago, but Brent had to remind himself that there were two women watching, including his sister, so he couldn't press Tristin against the truck and see if she still made those sexy little moans when he thrust deep inside her.

He pulled away, his lips swollen and numb and watched as she licked her lips once more. She slayed him. Every damn move she made absolutely slayed him.

"I give that a seven," Cyn said. "I think they can do better."

Courtney laughed. "I'm so not going there."

Right, audience. Brent stepped back, putting some distance between their bodies as he sucked in a deep breathe.

Tristin's smile had him wanting to move back in for more

though. "Do you need any help getting set up?" he asked.

With flushed cheeks, she shook her head. "I'm going to bring the bike down and then we'll get organized. Is the grocery store still in the same place?"

"It is. There's also a Super Wal-Mart now in Sunset Valley."

"Good to know."

He couldn't believe she was here, in Lilac Ridge, living on his property for the summer. There were so many things he wanted to do, wanted to share, wanted to talk about, but she'd been in town short of a couple hours and he was afraid his enthusiasm would scare her off.

"Do you two want to come down to the house for dinner tonight? I can grill up some chicken."

Tristin nodded. "That sounds good. I'm too exhausted to cook and I have a feeling Cyn is going to milk the broken foot for the rest of her life."

"Great. Come by around six."

She smiled and Brent took that as his cue to leave even though he didn't want to. Grabbing Court, he headed up the path to where they had both parked.

"She's cute," Courtney said. "I love how she knocked Bailey down a few pegs."

Tristin was more than cute, she was beautiful. Her fiery wit hadn't changed and while he wouldn't admit it, he had also enjoyed watching her knock Bailey down.

"You're eerily quiet," Courtney added.

Brent grunted even though he felt like jumping for joy like a little boy who had gotten everything he asked for on Christmas. Brent didn't know that feeling either, but he imagined it felt like this. "I'm trying to keep my cool," he admitted, but only because Courtney was his sister and she'd already figured that out anyway.

"Cyn is really cool. Hope you don't mind me offering the camping lot."

He didn't mind at all and wanted to hug her for it, but he

31

kept his cool about that too. "It's good."

When they reached the driveway, he gave his sister a playful shove and headed for his truck. Tristin's Harley was still parked on the edge of the gravel, but Court had plenty of room to get around it. When he got back to the house, he switched on the breaker and water valve for the camping lot and headed to the shop. It was hours until dinner, so he decided to keep himself busy with a carving.

No one had commissioned a bear, but it allowed the most work with the chain saw, providing the perfect distraction. Austin Hale had offered Brent a space at the upscale resort on Hale Mountain to showcase his carvings, so he needed to provide samples anyway.

Brent clapped on the ear muffs and slid on safety glasses before grabbing the sixteen inch chain saw. The chain was sharpened as part of his morning routine and he had several logs ready for carving, one already hoisted onto the hydraulic cart he used to save his back.

When he first started with the bear carvings, he marked the log with a loggers crayon so he knew where to cut. He still used that method with new or difficult carvings, but he'd been doing the bears so long, he didn't need the guidance.

He always started with the ears, then cut the angles for the nose, carving out the eyes as he did. It didn't take long to shape the log and while he could knock out the finer details a little faster, Brent liked to take his time. There was so much satisfaction in taking a regular old log and turning it into something more. Once he had the details flushed out, he put the chainsaw away and grabbed the blow torch. Some carvings he stained, but he preferred to burn the wood. It took skill to burn it just enough but not too much to get the right shadows and contrast.

By the time he was done, he'd worked up a good sweat. Brent stripped out of his t-shirt, tossing it in the pile with all the others covered in wood shavings. He hung them on the line and hosed them off before tossing them in the wash to save having to dig wood chips out of his washing machine.

"Whoa," he heard from behind him and spun around to find Tristin standing just inside the door.

Her eyes widened, a curious gaze shifting down his body before she shook her head, as if shaking herself out of a lustful daze.

A man could hope, anyway.

"You got new ink," she said, tilting her head as she studied his arms and shoulders.

His skin prickled with awareness as she studied one side and then the other. At nineteen, he already had ink on his left shoulder and upper arm, but the dragon on his left shoulder was new and so were the markings she couldn't see beneath his jeans. "They're amazing," she whispered.

Every hair stood on end, begging her fingers to trace over the designs, followed my her lips and tongue. Her gaze landed just below his navel, where the infinity tattoo that matched hers still took up residence.

"I kept it," he said. It was simple design, but spoke to the connection they shared that summer.

"I still have mine too," she said, and despite the sadness in her voice, the fact she still had the tattoo with his name sent a jolt from his heart to his cock.

"That bothers you?" he dared ask, taking a deep breath and bracing himself for her response.

Tristin shook her head. "Not at all, but it's a bit stretched," she paused, holding his gaze and taking in a deep breath, "from being pregnant."

"You have a child?" he spouted, unable to hide the surprise. Back at the pub she said she didn't, but pregnancy meant...

She shook her head. "I lost her. It's a story for another time." She turned and tugged her shirt up over her shoulders. "I got new ink too."

Brent had a million questions, but the sight of her inked skin made him weak in the knees. She was beautiful, her body

33

small and delicate, yet holding so much strength. "That's beautiful," he said, taking in the angel on her back.

"She's Tethys," Tristin said with an air of reverence in her voice. "She was a Greek sea goddess and the word nurse is derived from her name."

"She suits you," he said, his fingers twitching with the need to touch her. "I didn't realize Greek goddesses had wings."

"The wings are for my daughter, Angelica, because she's with the angels."

"How long?" he choked out.

"Almost five years. I'll tell you about it, but not today."

That wouldn't be long after she graduated from college if she stuck with the four year plan. "The father?" he asked, unable to let it go.

"We never married. The relationship didn't survive after she was lost."

"I'm sorry," he said, the pain on her face stabbing him in the gut.

"Thanks. It was a long time ago."

"Still tough, though."

"Yeah. I'm a nurse, so I'm smart enough to understand the medical reasons, but there's that maternal part of me that struggles with it."

He should step back, give her space, be a gentleman, but he wanted to take away her sadness, make her forget the tragedy she'd endured. "Understandable," he whispered.

She sighed, her mouth curving as the sadness left. "When you look at me like that, it's…" she licked her lips as the words trailed off.

"It's what, Tris?" he asked, moving closer.

"It's a nice distraction."

Brent wanted to be more than a distraction, but right now all he could think about was kissing her, pressing his bare chest against her body, holding her close.

She breathed another sigh, the kind that was all invitation. Brent accepted, lowering his mouth to hers. She turned her body toward his, her hands moving up his torso to his chest, where one rested against the rapid thump of his beating heart and the other circled around his nipple ring.

Naughty was the first word that came to mind, but that was nothing new. She'd been an open book when he'd known her so long ago, willing to do things most girls her age would never admit to even thinking about. He'd loved that about her, the wildness that couldn't be tamed, the way she embraced life at full speed.

Brent lifted her onto the work bench, settling between her legs. He wanted to take her, right here, right now, but he tamped the urge and focused on the kiss, the warmth of her mouth, the softness of her skin beneath his fingers.

Until someone coughed from the door between the shop and the house.

# Chapter 4

COULD SHE BUY a few minutes of privacy with the man who had lured her here with his heartfelt dedication and the memories of the summer they'd shared a lifetime ago?

Was a few minutes too much to ask? "I hate people," she muttered as Brent turned from her lips and looked over her shoulder.

"Um, sorry, but Darren is on the phone and says it's important," Courtney said.

"Whoa, wow," Cyn said a moment later. "Looks like you thawed the Ice Queen."

Tristin looked over her shoulder, finding Cyn peering over Courtney's shoulder — Courtney, who was looking anywhere but at an almost topless Tristin and a bare-chested Brent, caught in the clutches of the most amazing kiss in history. "Shut. Up," Tristin snarled. She loved Cyn, she really did, but sometimes…

"I'll call him back," Brent insisted.

"He said it's important," Courtney replied.

"And I said I'd call him back," Brent growled. "Give me a few minutes."

"Whatever," Courtney drawled and disappeared.

Cyn waggled her brow a few times. "Carry on," she chuckled, closing the door behind her.

Tristin breathed her frustration. "Sorry, I just came in to ask if I could use the shower, but you were carving and then you took off your shirt, and well, I kind of lost my mind."

"I always did like that about you."

"Right, because it never took much to talk you into any of my crazy ideas."

"I had a few crazy ideas of my own," he laughed.

"All of which I was totally on board with," she said. "You should go take your phone call."

"Yeah, right. The shower is yours. You'll find fresh towels in the bathroom closet. I have two water heaters, so you won't run out of hot water."

"Great. I was on the bike for four hours today. I wreak of the road."

"You smell great," he said, burying his face in her hair.

"So do you," she said, wrapping her arms and legs around his enticing body. She never knew the smell of man mixed with fresh-cut pine could be so arousing, but right now she wanted to bottle it up and bathe in it.

"You wreck me," he said, kissing her again.

Tristin let herself get lost in the kiss, the most thorough kiss she'd experienced since the last time she came to Lilac Ridge.

It had been hard to leave at the end of that summer. She'd cried for days in the car. At first her parents were sympathetic, and wouldn't even let her little brother, Troy tease her, but by the time they'd crossed the state line into Washington on their way to McChord Air Force Base, everyone had lost patience.

The tears dried up, but it was only when she'd started college that she was able to move on.

Brent nuzzled her neck, planting sweet kisses under her

chin, behind her ear, oh God, she wanted so much more.

"I love that sound you make. Makes me forget everything except I'm a man and you're all woman."

She locked her ankles behind him, pulling him closer. She slid to the edge of the table, his erection pressed to her core, the heat exploding between them.

"Yes," she whispered, feeling the same. She wanted him, just as much as she had all those years ago…maybe even more.

Brent groaned against her neck. "We need to slow down before this gets out of control."

"I don't want to slow down. I'm only here for the summer and I don't want to waste a minute of it."

Three thumps at the door had Brent sighing.

"Darren's on his way over," Courtney yelled.

"Shit," Brent muttered, echoing Tristin's sentiment. She didn't know who this Darren person was, but right now, she didn't like him all that much.

Brent tugged her shirt down. "I can do better than a work bench with constant interruptions from the peanut gallery," he said.

She didn't care where they were, but the constant interruptions were a problem. "I look forward to it," she said, tracing her hand down his torso. He was strong, a body forged from hard work. Tristin felt like the girl she'd once been, wild and free, and desperate to be alone and naked with this man.

"I need to go grab a clean shirt," he muttered. With his hands braced on her thighs, he made no attempt to move.

"Shame. I like the view." She tugged on his nipple rings, pulling another groan from him. "I like these piercings, too."

"I like your hands on me, but I need to get dressed."

"Who is Darren?" she asked.

"He's a friend. He's engaged to Maddie."

"Really?" she asked. Tristin was looking forward to seeing Maddie and Clarissa. Way back when, they were fun, a little crazy too, so she fit right in with them.

"Yeah. They're getting married in August. I'm the best man."

The thought of Brent in a tux had her mouth watering. "So you and Darren are close?" she asked.

"Yeah. He's from Sunset Valley, bought the stables here."

"He had to be a horse guy for Maddie to marry him. She was crazy about horses."

"Still is. She's starting up an equine assisted therapy center with Clarissa and Darren. Clarissa's a veterinarian. Maddie's a psychotherapist."

"Wow. That's great. I still imagine everyone in their teens, but I guess we all grew up." So far, she liked the grown-up Brent. She'd only spent minutes with him, but first impressions were important and he'd made a good one. His looks didn't hurt, or that spark they still shared.

"Do you mind if I look around at your carvings?" she asked.

"Have at it," he said. "Enjoy your shower."

Brent kissed her forehead before stepping off and going through the door that Courtney and Cyn had peeked through a few minutes ago.

The carvings were amazing. He had several bears standing against one wall, all various sizes. A pair of dolphins stood together, their finish smooth, the poses playful. Smaller carvings of woodland animals included a rabbit, a raccoon, and a fox. There was a large eagle, wings angled behind it, that took her breath away.

When a truck pulled up outside, Tristin's curiosity got the better of her. Did Brent's friend know about her? Would Brent tell him she was there?

Voices hummed from inside the house as she stepped through the door from his shop. She walked with careful steps to try and catch any conversation, but they seemed to be talking about a tree that had fallen.

"Maddie convinced Dave Hamilton to let you clear it," the other man said.

Brent chuckled. "I find that hard to believe. Does he want me to pay him for the wood?"

"No. Maddie appealed to his tight wallet. If you remove the tree, it doesn't cost Hamilton a dime. Otherwise, he has to pay someone to do it because we both know he's not going to lift a finger."

"Hamilton doesn't make anything that easy. There must be conditions," Brent said.

"A couple," his friend responded.

"All right, hit me."

"First, it has to be gone today."

"That's a big tree," Brent grunted.

"You've got me, and Maddie's dad offered to help too. Maddie said she'd call Coop, see if he's free. We should be able to manage it."

"And the second condition?"

The guy laughed now. "He wants you to stay away from Bailey."

Bailey…that was the woman from the pub, the one who tried to warn Tristin away from Brent.

Brent chuckled. "That ship sailed a long time ago."

Tristin was relieved to hear that, the rising jealousy dispersing before it ever took hold. She didn't have a right to be jealous since she was only here for the summer, but she wanted Brent all to herself and did not want to share him with that Stepford wife wannabe.

"For you, yeah, but not for Bailey."

Tristin moved around the corner. Brent's back was to her, but the other guy looked at her, and that drew Brent's attention too. "Sorry, I was eavesdropping," she admitted. "I can help with the tree."

"Darren Brown, meet Tristin May," Brent said.

The man's eyes widened. "Tristin? *The* Tristin?"

Tristin stepped forward and extended her hand. "In the flesh."

"Welcome back to Lilac Ridge," Darren said, offering a

firm handshake. "When did you get here?"

"A couple hours ago."

"Aw, shit, man, sorry," Darren muttered, turning back to Brent. "I can let Hamilton know you can't deal with the tree today."

"Is this for your carvings?" Tristin asked.

"Yeah. A big old oak is blocking a parking lot behind an office building in town. If I remove it, the logs are mine."

"Then what are we waiting for?" she asked.

Brent's smile motivated her even more. "Right. Let me recruit Courtney too. I imagine there's going to be a lot of branches to deal with. I think she's up at your RV with Cyn."

"I'll go get them. You get whatever you need and we'll meet you at the end of the driveway."

"A woman who takes charge. I like her," Darren said. "I'll help with the equipment."

With all the logs stacked under the car port next to Brent's shop and all branches piled near the wood chipper, Brent was ready for a long, hot shower. Since Tristin had been ready for one before they headed out to deal with the tree, he wondered if she was game for a little co-ed washing.

He'd be happy to wash her back and any other part she wanted him to handle. She didn't even have to return the favor. Except naked shower time would lead to other naked activities and Brent didn't want to rush into things.

"You're thinking dirty thoughts," she said, hopping up on the tailgate next to him with the grace of a ballerina. That's how she'd worked on the tree, too, with strength and skill that had shocked him given her size.

"Always," he drawled. "You bring out the dirty in me."

"Some things never change," she laughed. The sound

tugged him back to that summer when her laughter was the only thing that broke up his dirty thoughts.

Brent brushed aside a rogue blonde wisp from her cheek, the softness of her skin inviting him to kiss her. She let out one of those sexy little sighs as her arms moved around his waist. He loved her hands on him, her body against his. Everything about Tristin stole his breath.

"I need a shower," he murmured against her mouth as her hands slid beneath his shirt.

"Is that an invitation?"

Jesus, how could he say no? Except he didn't just want to throw her in bed and have his way with her. Okay, he did, but that wasn't the sole or immediate purpose of his intentions. He'd made that dedication because he wanted more than just a satisfying roll. A gentleman would take the time to get to know her first. It didn't matter that the last ten years had been erased the moment she walked back into his life. The fact was, those years did exist and they had both changed.

"Maybe we should wait," he suggested.

Tristin raised a single eyebrow. "Wait for what?"

"We shouldn't jump into anything, you know, too quickly."

That eyebrow remained arched, her head shaking. "It's not like we're strangers. We've been together before."

"Right, but we were kids and that was a decade ago."

"So," she drawled.

"So, I want to get to know you again, take you on a date, show you the respect you deserve."

She laughed now and Brent swallowed the lump rising in his throat. "What joke did I miss?"

"I'm sorry, I shouldn't laugh. You're just so different. I mean, yeah, I guess I am too, but, I don't know, you seem a bit conservative. I wasn't expecting that."

He'd been called aloof, stubborn, even hard-headed, but never conservative. "I'm not conservative," he mumbled.

She moved across his body, straddling his thighs. Every nerve ending fired up, all the blood rushing out of his head. "If you don't want me, just say so."

The teasing sound of her voice warned him not to take the bait, but Brent wasn't one to play games. "I want you."

Her playful smile sparked with the same desire he continued to battle. "Then let's not waste time or water." She pushed off his body, standing and holding out her hand. Brent took it and stood, following as she took the lead and headed for the house.

When they reached the front door, a blood-curdling scream echoed through the trees. "Cyn," Tristin sighed with a roll of her eyes. "What kind of wild animals do you have here?"

"A little of everything. You didn't leave any garbage out, did you?"

"No, we know better. I better check on her."

"Hang on, let me grab the rifle." Brent preferred to live peacefully with all the animals that occupied the woods on and around his property, but if bears milled about, especially a mother and cubs, he wouldn't hesitate to fire a warning shot to scare them away from the camper.

His gun safe was bolted to the wall in the closet just inside the front door. He entered the code, grabbed the .22, and was back by Tristin's side in under a minute.

"That's a mighty big gun you have," she teased.

"If you think this is big, you should see my shot gun," he teased back.

"I thought I was about to. I'm going to kill her if she's screaming about nothing."

A path led them through the woods to the camper, a shorter route than taking the driveway. When they made it into the clearing, Cyn stood on the picnic table near the camper wearing nothing but a towel.

"What's going on?" Tristin asked.

"I came out of the shower and he was in there, rustling around in a drawer. He ran under the bunks."

"Who is he?" Tristin asked.

"A trash-panda. Oh, God, I'm going to get rabies."

"Did it bite you?" Tristin asked.

"No, but it could. How did it get in there? The door was latched."

"What the hell is a trash-panda?" Brent cut in.

"A raccoon," Tristin informed him.

"Shit. That's Rascal." He unloaded the gun and handed it to Tristin, tucking the bullets into his pocket as he made for the camper.

"Rascal?" Cyn asked. "Who are you, Pocahontas?"

It wasn't the first time Brent had been accused of being the Disney princess, despite the fact he wasn't a woman and the raccoon he'd rescued as a mere babe on the side of the road wasn't named Meeko.

Brent left the camper door open after he stepped in so Rascal could leave of her own accord. He found the critter in the sink, nibbling on a graham cracker.

"Hey, girl," he said. "Causing trouble?"

Her high-pitched chirp let him know she was happy and didn't care what kind of trouble she may have caused. When she finished the cracker, Brent held out his finger. Rascal wrapped a paw around it, their own secret handshake. "How about we take these outside?"

He knew the raccoon well enough to know she wouldn't leave the crackers behind. If he forced her to, she'd be back inside the camper before the night was over. He supposed it was his fault. After he'd rescued her, graham crackers were the only thing he had around that seemed safe to give her. He'd eventually bought a bag of dog food, but graham crackers worked as a special treat. She lived in the wild, but Brent made sure he kept both dog food and graham crackers on hand — tightly sealed and locked up, of course — just to be sure she didn't go hungry.

"You have a pet raccoon?" Tristin asked, once again sneaking up on him.

He gazed over his shoulder, Tristin's amused smirk making his heart race even more. "I rescued her, but she lives in the wild."

With the crackers in hand, he took two steps toward the door, but Tristin didn't make room for him to pass. Her smile spoke volumes, but Brent had heard it all before.

"Don't do that," he said before she could say anything.

"Do what?" she chuckled.

"Tell me how sweet it is, what a hero I am, ya-da, ya-da, ya-da."

"But it is sweet and I'm sure Rascal here thinks you're a hero."

"Anyone would have done it."

"I doubt that."

Brent shook the crackers, prompting rascal to follow and Tristin to back down the steps. When the critter hit the ground, Brent latched the door. "She likes graham crackers. I suggest you don't keep them in the camper." He broke off a piece and handed it to the little beggar. Rascal nibbled away without a care in the world.

Cyn continued to stand on the picnic table, her breaths on the verge of hyperventilating.

"She's not going to bother you," he said.

"Don't care."

"She was bitten a few years ago," Tristin said. "Had to have the preventative shots."

"By a raccoon?" Brent asked.

"A bat," Cyn snarled.

"We've got those out here too," he warned. "But I've never had a problem with them."

Cyn grunted and waved a hand as if shooing Rascal away. "You can make your little friend go into the woods now."

"I'll entice her away, remind her where the goods are." Brent looked at Tristin, hoping to pick up where they left off.

"I better stay here. She'll never calm down on her own." Brent nodded, trying to hide his disappointment despite being the one who said they should wait. Maybe it was for the best. He didn't want to rush into anything, wanted Tristin to see him

45

for the responsible man he was, not the reckless boy he used to be.

~ ♥ ~

After an hour of tossing and turning and watching the dim glow of the moon move around his bedroom, Brent couldn't continue to torment himself. His chainsaw offered a welcome reprieve, but at midnight, it would wake Courtney, if not Tristin and Cyn.

Instead, he opted to chop firewood. It didn't require a whole lot of concentration, something he couldn't muster when every single brain cell remained zeroed in on Tristin.

With each clap of the ax through an eighteen inch log, the wood pile grew. If he got through all the logs, he'd get to stacking, another mindless task that would wear his body down until it had no choice but to sleep.

"Can't sleep?" Tristin asked as he propped up another log.

Brent chuckled. "Not many people can sneak up on me like that."

"I wasn't trying to," she said, taking a seat on one of the uncut logs.

"I didn't wake you, did I?"

Tristin shook her head, a smile curving her pretty mouth. "No. I was watching the stars, recognized the sound of an ax chopping wood. Knew it had to be you."

Brent put the ax down and claimed the spot next to Tristin on the log, looking up at the sparkling sky. "See anything interesting up there?" he asked.

"No shooting stars, but without a moon, the stars are brilliant tonight."

Brent didn't spend a lot of time looking up, but he couldn't disagree. The black canvas lay in stark contrast to the twinkling lights spackled across the sky.

"What's got you up?" he asked.

"I'm a night owl," she said. "And Cyn snores like a grizzly when she's had a few drinks. There's no falling asleep to that music. What's got you up?"

Brent shrugged.

"That's all I get, a shrug? Are we going to have to play the truth game?" she laughed.

"The truth game? That's a little juvenile, don't you think?" he chuckled, nudging her shoulder.

"It's a mechanism for communication, which is a very adult thing."

"This is where I warn you about what you wish for. Sometimes the truth is more than you bargained for."

"I can handle it," she advised.

Brent weighed the pros and cons of being honest. She'd just gotten into town and he didn't want to come across as a lovestruck pussy, but he didn't want her to think he let his dick run his life.

"I was thinking about you."

"Oh yeah. What kind of thoughts?" she teased

"The kind that'll get me in trouble."

"Well, if it's any consolation, I was having those kind of thoughts, too." Her finger traced an erotic design over his thigh. The thoughts he'd been trying to purge from his brain earlier surged back in as all the blood rushed from his head to below his waist.

"Just so we're clear, exactly what were your thoughts?" he asked. Tristin's body beneath him hadn't been the only thing keeping him up. She'd dropped a bomb earlier, about being pregnant and Brent might lose his mind thinking about what had happened.

"You tell me yours and I'll tell you mine," she said.

"I'm afraid if I tell you mine, you'll run for the hills."

She shook her head, those fingers still making his body insane with need. "I'm not the same girl you knew all those years ago, but at the core, I haven't changed all that much. I'm still an open book."

Tristin had been just like that the summer they'd been together. Not only did she put it all out there, but she kept an open mind. She'd been receptive to all his pent-up angst, giving him a much-needed outlet. That had been all about his parents, though. Since she was now the catalyst for all his emotions, he wasn't sure if she'd be so receptive.

"I never told you I loved you that summer," he said, copping out of the here and now.

She looked at him, her brow raised, a smirk tilting her lips. "No, you didn't."

"I did. Love you, that is. I just didn't know how to put it to words. Didn't think it mattered."

"I was leaving at the end of the summer. Those words wouldn't have changed that."

"I know. I think that's why I didn't say it."

Now she narrowed her eyes. "Is that what's keeping you up? The fact you didn't say you loved me when you were nineteen?"

Brent shook his head. "No."

In a move that had his head spinning, she threw a leg over his thighs, straddling him as her hands landed on his chest. She kept her weight off him, the space an erotic tease that had him planting his hands on her hips and pulling her all the way down.

Her naughty smile pressed against his lips, offering a quick tease before her mouth opened and she traced her tongue across his lips.

She was still assertive, one of the many things he had fallen in love with, but now it threatened to whisk away all of his good intentions.

"Tell me," she whispered against his lips.

"You think I can form a coherent thought that doesn't involve one or both of us naked right now?"

"One?" she teased, intrigue arching one eyebrow.

"There are so many ways I want to explore your body," he

48

admitted since she was looking for honesty. "Some of them don't require me to be undressed."

"Promise?"

The woman slayed him, but despite every instinct pushing him to take her right out here in the wild, he hunkered down and focused on the other half of what kept him awake. "I promise, but first thing's first. I want to know about you. Ten years feels like a lifetime and you said some things that have my head spinning."

"Right. You want to know about my daughter."

Brent nodded as the playfulness left her smile. A part of him didn't want to know. Ignorance was bliss, after all, and Tristin having a daughter meant she'd been with other men, or at least one. The thought raised his hackles, but he reminded himself that he'd been with other women. They had parted ways so long ago, with no plans to ever see each other again. She obviously hadn't been pining after him all this time.

"If it's too soon—" he started.

"I want to tell you, and I promise I will, but not tonight."

# Chapter 5

THE THERAPISTS ENCOURAGED Tristin to talk about what had happened, said it would help her work through the pain and move on.

Back then, she didn't want to move on and all these years later, talking about it still poured fuel on the pain.

She was ashamed of what she'd done, abandoning a man she was supposed to love on their wedding day, and how she'd handled losing Angelica. Her shame hadn't stopped there. She'd escaped to Vegas, gone on a bender to end all benders, and ended up at a chapel, about to marry a man she didn't even know.

And for the second time in as many months, she left a man at the altar.

"I did things I'm not proud of," she admitted without offering details, praying Brent wouldn't ask for them.

"We've all done things we aren't proud of. You just gotta learn from it."

"I have," she said, swiping at the tears. She thought things through now, on her own, without outside pressure.

"I didn't want to come here," she admitted. "I mean, I did. I wanted to see you, but, it's temporary. It's just the summer."

She turned to face him, pushing aside the shame she still lived with and the regret that she would hurt him before the summer was over. "It's just the summer, Brent, and I don't want to waste a single moment."

Tearing the shirt over her head, she closed the distance between them, scraping her fingernails down his firm chest and ripped torso. His skin was hot, a burning fire beneath her fingertips.

She tore his shirt over his head too, but despite the growl, he didn't stop her. "I want you, so much," she confessed.

"I don't have a condom, anywhere, I'm—"

"I've got it covered." Tristin fumbled with his button fly, only to have his hands clutching hers before she could finish.

"How do you have it covered?"

"Check my back pocket."

His hand moved across her ass, reaching into the pocket and pulling the condom out.

"Jesus, Tris, I—"

"Don't say no."

"How could I?" he said, his voice so thick and his eyes so fierce she knew he wanted this as much as she did.

Without any further argument, his hands moved up and released the clasp of her bra with the deftness of a surgeon, once again growling as he eased the straps and cups off her body.

"So beautiful," he murmured, inspiring her to get back to work on that button fly.

He was just as skilled with her cargo pants, stripping her down before she managed to work all the buttons on his pants. He put the condom in her hand and took over, pushing his jeans down and stepping out of them as she did the same. A light from the side of the house illuminated the space, giving her a clear view of every inch of ink.

"Wow," she said. His hips and thighs hadn't been graced with any art all those years ago. She wanted to know the story behind the dragon on his bicep and shoulder and the intricate patterns below his waist, but now was not the time for time for talking.

"You looking at my ink or something else?"

Her gaze shifted to his, where that fire burned. "Yes," she said, tearing the condom open and stepping up to him. "How are we going to…"

The corner of his lips lifted into the smirk that showed a man who knew just what he wanted and how to get it. "I got this."

While rolling the condom over his thick and hot length, his very male and primal groan made her eager to see how he was going to work his magic.

Brent pulled her against him, leaning down to claim her mouth. His strong arms cocooned her, his body hard and hot against hers, cranking up the heat under the cool midnight air. His hands moved down, cupping her ass and lifting her like she weighed nothing.

"I should do you right and take you to bed, make love to you like you deserve."

"You should shut up and take me right here, right now."

Tristin had always been petite and Brent had always been big and strong. Her size hadn't changed at all since they were young, but he'd gotten bigger, stronger, sexier. He positioned her hips right…there…pulling her down and driving into her.

Bending her knees so her feet and ankles pushed against his thighs for leverage, she folded her hands together behind his neck for stability, hanging on with every ounce of strength, loving the erotic connection.

"Yes," she pleaded, desperate for more. How he was able to piston in and out of her was a testament to his strength and it made her burn even hotter.

It was the ultimate free fall, feeling Brent inside her, holding her with those strong, beautiful arms. Nothing else mattered, not the past, not the future, just the here, the now, the two of them.

~ ♥ ~

Brent couldn't get enough of Tristin, wrapped around him, hanging on with surprising strength as the last ten years of being alone took hold. He wanted to make love to her slowly, to revel in her silken flesh, in every soft, feminine curve of her beautiful body, but the moment he found the condom in her pocket, he lost all patience and control.

She weighed nothing and was so perfect in his arms, her breaths hitching with her pleasure, clinging to him as he pushed in, deeper and deeper.

And every time his name crossed her lips, he lost a little more control.

"Tris," he groaned as her cries came faster and louder, as she hung on tighter. Thinking about chainsaws did nothing to tamp his desire and thank God he got her there first. As her body became a vice grip around his, Brent dug his fingers into her perfect ass, hoping to hell he didn't drop her as they reached the euphoria he'd missed all these years.

Despite the cool summer air, their bodies now glistened with sweat. As she came back from her release, her eyes opened, a beautiful and satisfied smile lifting her cheeks and brightening her pretty green eyes.

When his lungs stopped huffing, he rested his forehead against hers. "I wanted to be a gentleman, give us time to get to know each other again, but hell, Tris, that was…"

She placed a finger across his lips. "I'm only here for the summer," she said again, the words a dull, jagged knife piercing his heart. "I don't want to waste a second of it, Brent. Not a single second."

He didn't want to waste a second either, but that radio

show dedication wasn't about just a summer, it was about seeing if they had a future.

"I must be getting heavy," she said, kissing his shoulder.

His thighs might be screaming for a reprieve after their little workout, but Brent wasn't ready to concede. "I could hold you like this forever."

"Still a sweet talker." Her smile cranked up his pulse a few beats. "It's okay to put me down."

He didn't want to, but he did, just to give her arms and legs a break. While she seemed to enjoy the midnight air, making no move to put her clothes back on, he took care of the condom, wrapping it up in some old newspaper and putting it in the trashcan next to the woodshed.

Once again, he closed the distance between them, pulling her lithe body flush to his. "Stay with me," he insisted, his arms going around her, "so we don't waste a minute."

Looking up at him, she smiled, her eyes giving him the answer he needed, but her words filling his heart. "I'd love to stay with you."

He scooped her into his arms, abandoning their clothes and heading to the house. Tristin giggled the whole way. As they crossed the kitchen, a light brightened from the doorway at the end of the hall.

Well, shit. "Don't come out here, Court," he warned, not wanting to give his sister a show that could scar her for life.

Of course, his little sister didn't listen, coming out of the room, uttering a colorful string of curses, and spinning around to head back in. When the door slammed, Tristin giggled even more. "She's going to hate me," Tristin said, though the playfulness in her voice contradicted the worry in her words.

He didn't have any condoms, and based on her nakedness, she wasn't hiding anymore either, but he planned to spend the whole night showing her that the summer wasn't enough time.

~ ♥ ~

Brent woke up with a painful case of morning wood and an empty bed. He scrubbed the sleep away and looked around, but there was no sign of Tristin. When did she sneak out? And how? He wasn't a sound sleeper, but the last thing he remembered was her curled up against his body in the dark of night. Now, the open curtains let in the morning light, leaving no indication night had ever been there.

He tugged on jeans and headed out of the room, the unmistakable smell of bacon wafting up the stairs. When he reached the kitchen, he found Tristin in his shirt, hovering over the stove.

"Morning," he murmured, coming up behind her. The room smelled like bacon, but she smelled like a mountain breeze after the rain. Brent wanted to wrap himself up with her.

"Good morning. Did you sleep well?" she turned only her head and planted a sweet kiss to his cheek.

"Like the dead. I didn't hear you get up."

"You didn't even stir, so I didn't want to wake you. Figured you'd be up for bacon and eggs, though."

He and Courtney took turns making dinner, but it was only on rare occasions when one of them cooked breakfast. "I'm always up for bacon and eggs."

When the bacon was done, she broke a couple eggs in the pan. Brent dropped two slices of bread in the toaster while he waited and when the toast popped, Tristin served up his eggs and bacon. "This might give you a heart attack," she warned.

"I usually have raisin bran in the morning, so I think I'm safe."

She cooked two more eggs, handling the toast on her own. Brent should have helped, but the grumble in his stomach demanded he enjoy the breakfast hot.

Funny, that's how he enjoyed Tristin too.

"You have that look," she laughed, taking a seat adjacent to him at the small farmhouse table.

"The look of a very satisfied man?" he asked.

"The look of a very horny man."

"Yeah, well, I woke up ready for more, but I didn't have a beautiful, naked woman next to me to take the edge off."

"Okay, note to self, wake up sexy, naked man before I get out of bed."

Brent liked that idea. It was the kind of morning wake-up he could get used to without even trying. He shoveled the rest of his breakfast in and used the toast to sop up all the yolk and bacon grease left on the plate.

"That's clean enough to put back in the cupboard," Tristin laughed.

"I am my own dishwasher. Just don't tell Courtney."

"Don't tell Courtney what?" his sister said as she came into the kitchen.

"Do you want me to make you a couple eggs?" Tristin asked, saving him.

"Nah, I'm trying this detox thing. Fruit only for me until lunch. Then I get vegetables. Yum." Court didn't need to lose weight so he didn't understand this trendy new diet she was trying, but who was he to tell a woman how or what to eat. That just meant more bacon for him.

He washed his plate and the pan Tristin used, then washed her very clean plate when she finished. They both picked at the few slices of bacon left over.

"What's your plan today?" he asked.

"Hiking. You game?"

Another thing that hadn't changed about Tristin, her need for adventure. Brent would prefer to spend the day with her wrapped around him, but he did want to get to know her again and a day hiking seemed a great way to do that. "Yeah, I'm game."

# Chapter 6

TRISTIN DIDN'T MIND the heat, but she'd forgotten how unforgiving the humidity in New Hampshire could be. Brent, though, he lived here, so it made no sense that he was dragging ass behind her.

"How can a guy who looks as fit as you be sucking wind so hard?" she asked when he joined her at the end of the trail.

"I wield a chainsaw. It doesn't require the lung capacity that this hill does."

"You don't still smoke, do you?" she asked. It was one of the stupid things they'd done the summer they'd spent together.

"No, gave it up when I gave up drinking."

"Good," she said, moving up on her toes to kiss him. If the sexy growl he made didn't encourage her to run her tongue across his lips, the way he gripped her hips would have. Her hands slid down his sinewy arms, memorizing the trail of veins that testified to his strength. She slid across his stomach, tugging at this shirt and moving up his firm skin to the rings through his nipples.

"Jesus," he cursed against her mouth.

He was damp with sweat and she was about to pass out from the heat. "Let's go for a dip," she suggested.

Stepping back from his enticing body, she stripped out of her shirt and shorts, down to her simple black bra and black panties.

"Jesus," he muttered again.

"Going to join me?" she asked, moving to the water.

"This is a public place. Anyone could come up here."

"And that's why we're not skinning dipping." That had been her first inclination when she'd chosen the trail for their hike, but she wasn't as reckless as the teen Brent had known. While Tristin loved an adventure, she prided herself on being responsible, not reckless.

Mostly.

Once the water reached her knees, she dove in, loving how the ice-cold lake cooled her body with its frigid depths.

Coming up for air, she found Brent stripping out of his jeans, his boots already placed on a big rock.

"Be prepared for shrinkage," she warned after honing in on the large bulge in his tight-fitting boxer briefs.

"Great," he muttered, but didn't hesitate. No, he barreled right in, diving much the way she did. He came up right next to where she was treading.

"Shit, that's cold."

"Told you," she laughed. Brent had a good five inches on her, so he could stand, the water reaching his chin. Tristin wrapped herself around him, his body heat seeping into her flesh without any regard for the ice-cold mountain lake. Brent shifted, moving them into shallower water where the steam rolled off their skin in the mid-day sun.

"Tell me about the piercings," she said, her pert nipples brushing against them.

"A reminder to stay the course," he said, kissing her chin, her neck, zeroing in on that special spot below her ear.

"Stay the course?" she asked. In just the twenty-four hours they'd spent together, she noted how much he'd changed. He was reserved now, calm, not the wild boy she'd loved. Not that he wasn't great, because so far she'd enjoyed every second with him, but the piercings and tattoos still spoke of the crazy teen he'd been.

He held on to her, but stopped kissing, his gaze intense, serious — too serious. "I drank. A lot. Too much." Shaking his head, he broke the stare, looking up at the sky.

"Tell me," she encouraged.

"I'd drink, drive, didn't give a shit about anyone, not even myself. In hindsight, I think I was seeking an early grave. Almost got my wish. I clipped another car one night, rolled the Jeep, spent some time in the hospital and in court. Thank God no one else was hurt, but it was a wake-up call, you know, scared me sober."

"Oh," she said, tryin not to judge him for the mistakes he made. Though he straddled the line between right and wrong back when she knew him — and so did she — he was kind and generous, the kind of person who would go to bat for anyone he cared about.

Tristin reminded herself what he'd done had nothing to do with what she'd survived. He wasn't to blame for her accident and her daughter's death.

That didn't keep the anger from bubbling up and festering in her throat. Logic couldn't extinguish the fire in her chest because the source ran too deep. That kind of pain and anger always smoldered.

Brent shook his head, concentrating on the sky again. "I'm not proud of it, haven't had a drink since."

"How long ago?" she asked.

"Eight years."

"Wow," he was so young.

"I got my shit together after that, focused on being a better person. Well, I'm still working on that."

He was hurting, that was clear. She recognized it because

she still hurt too. Cupping his chin with one hand, Tristin waited for his gaze to shift back to her. He abandoned his search of the sky and looked at her. She pushed aside her own angst, rooting in for the affection that also burned for this man, and the compassion that always settled her soul. "I figured it was more of a masochistic thing."

"Only when you touch them," he groaned as she tugged one of the piercings. "I don't deserve this, you."

"Sshhhh," she said, pressing a finger over his lips. The regret in his eyes broke her heart. She didn't have the words to comfort him, to offer the forgiveness he sought because it wasn't hers to offer. "What about this?" she asked, tracing the dragon on his right arm. It had an infinity symbol in it, a symbol that had been theirs the summer they spent together. They both knew their time together was short back then, but the symbol was to remind them the memories would never die.

"Another reminder that my demons are only a breath away. Some days they are easier to ignore than others."

As a nurse, Tristin had seen plenty of devastation caused by alcoholism. Brent had been raised in the trenches, so it was no surprise he fought a constant battle, but the man who held her was strong, resilient. He'd survived his childhood and from what she'd seen, had come out of his own tragedy a better man.

She didn't have any reassuring words, not when her own demons lingered only a breath away. Before they could take hold, she pressed her mouth to Brent's. Eliciting one of his sexy little groans, she moved her hips, bringing that very erotic part of him back to life. Brent's hands gripped her ass, squeezing and pulling as she continued to grind against him.

"Fuck," he groaned.

Yes, hell, yes, that's what she wanted, but the condom she'd packed was in her backpack on shore.

"We need to get the condom," she said, attempting to pull away. His grip on her ass tightened.

"No. I want to watch you get off like this," he growled,

hunger flashing across his eyes.

*This* was the Brent she remembered. They'd had plenty of quickies as teens, but most of the time, he was more concerned with her pleasure than his own. She'd been with adult men who didn't have that kind of focus.

Without argument, she moved with his hands, pressing harder against him, sliding up and down the erection still restrained within his boxers.

Every inch of her skin came to life, the tingle starting right at the center of her universe and traveling at the speed of light to everywhere. "Brent," she whispered, sure her eyes had rolled to the back of her head.

"That's it, Tris. Ride me."

She wanted more, needed more, but without a condom and with two layers of underwear, all she could do was lock her ankles behind him to get even closer as…she…got closer.

"Touch me," she pleaded, and one hand left her ass to tug the cup of her bra aside. His tongue flicked her nipple, the warmth a shock against her cold skin, one that pushed her out of orbit.

Rocking against him and crying out, his tongue was relentless, pushing her further and further into a tailspin. Every muscle contracted, greedy and hungry, looking for some piece of him to cling to.

"You are so fucking hot."

She didn't even take a moment to come back down before reaching inside his boxers, wrapping her hand around his hot, velvet skin. "You're turn."

Voices echoed up the path, stilling both of them. "We better get dressed before we have an audience," he grumbled, pulling her hand from him.

Before she could suggest that they swim out into the lake for privacy, Brent was tugging her toward land. They dressed with less speed than they'd disrobed since their skin was wet, but managed to get everything on before a family of five hit the clearing. The three boys cheered, shoes flying as they charged toward the water. Splashing commenced, giving Tristin and Brent their queue to leave.

"That was close," he muttered, holding her hand while leading her down the path.

Tristin snagged the lead, almost dragging him down the three miles of ruddy, rooted, rocky trail back to the truck. It was the fastest trip down a mountain she'd ever had, Brent chuckling as she pushed him inside the truck and climbed on top of him.

"What are you doing?" he asked while she tore at the buttons on his jeans.

"It's your turn," she repeated, desperate to make him come with the same intensity she'd experienced.

He was hard again, or still — whichever, it didn't matter — and without preamble, she lowered her mouth to him.

The grumbled curses echoed in the truck, egging her on. She teased and sucked, playing with the tip and taking him in as far as she could. His hands wove into her hair, keeping her positioned right where he liked her, making her burn even hotter for him.

She wanted to make this about him, but he was so damn hot and despite the intensity of the orgasm in the lake, she had missed the feel of him inside her. Stripping out of her shorts and panties with little grace because the truck didn't offer a whole lot of room, she fumbled with her backpack before he grabbed it.

"Front pocket," she directed and without taking his eyes off her, he unzipped the pocket and found the condom, tearing it open and rolling it on.

Squealing as he flipped her over, quite a feat in the cramped space, Tristin braced her hands against the passenger door as he moved on top of her. His pants were still around his thighs, but he didn't seem to care, driving home with a solid thrust.

"Jesus, yes," he groaned and pushed her shirt up, this time flicking the front clasp. Her breasts spilled out, eager for attention. Brent obliged, his mouth claiming one, his hand the other.

"I'm going to come," he declared against her skin, the last audible word before she was coming too, her muscles finding that piece of him to cling to in erotic desperation and release.

~ ♥ ~

Since his pants never made it past his knees, it didn't take long to get himself tucked back in, all the while thinking about when he could get Tristin naked again. "One of these days I'll do right by you and take you to bed," he muttered.

"No complaints from me," she said, pulling on her clothes. "That was the last condom though."

Since he hadn't had sex in ages, he didn't have a stash. If he'd known Tristin was going to show up, he would have been prepared. He'd never been a Boy Scout, but appreciated their motto. "I need to hit the store for steaks, anyway. Have dinner with me?"

"I'd love to."

Sweet music to his ears.

With all clothing in place, he found the keys and got the truck moving before he was tempted to take her right there in the front seat again.

Tristin sang along to the radio as they made their way back to Lilac Ridge, every off-key note tightening the bond on his heart. She hadn't changed, not much, still carefree and living life to the fullest, even in the simplicity of singing along with a song.

When they reached the grocery store, she held his hand walking through the parking lot, their arms swinging with a natural ease, as if they'd always been together.

Maybe a part of them had.

"How about we divide and conquer. The faster we get

back, the faster we can eat, and the faster you can take me to bed."

Brent was on board with that idea. With a nod, he grabbed a basket and headed into the store. "I'll grab the steaks. Courtney keeps the fridge stocked with salad fixings, but do you want to grab a more substantial side?"

"Rock-n-roll," she chirped, planting a kiss to his lips before skipping off. He rubbed his chest, trying to calm his heart as it flipped over and over. She was so beautiful and fun and Brent didn't want to be away from her for a second, so he rushed to the other end of the store, grabbing the best-looking steak tips he could find. Next stop, the condom aisle.

He shouldn't have been surprised to find Tristin already there, perusing the selection. "Fancy meeting you here," she chuckled.

"I like a woman with initiative," he said. "What's your pleasure?"

"Well, if we're thinking of me, there's always ribbed for her pleasure, but if we're thinking of you, we should probably get the extra large."

"You're good for my ego," he laughed. "Get what you like." Condoms were a necessary evil, though he didn't mind the feel of her hand as she rolled one on him last night, but he couldn't stop the fantasy playing in his head, of taking her with no protection, coming inside her as she cried his name, making her his, not just for one night or the summer, but for the rest of their lives.

She grabbed a box of each variety, tossing them in her basket with the veggies she'd collected.

"Well, aren't you two cozy," Bailey muttered behind them.

Brent rolled his eyes, taking a deep breath as they turned, but before he could say something polite, Tristin took charge.

"Bailey, right?" she said in a sickly sweet voice.

"Right," Bailey muttered again, scowl firmly in place.

"So good to see you again. What brings you to the condom aisle?"

Brent suppressed the chuckle as anger, maybe disgust flared in Bailey's eyes.

"I'm not, ugh, some people." She peered into Tristin's basket, her lip curling when she saw all the condoms. "In town one night and already sleeping together? Kind of slutty, don't you think? I made him wait two months."

"Two months? Wow, no wonder you're so uptight. Here," Tristin pulled a box of the ribbed condoms out of the basket and dropped them in Bailey's. "Wrap one of these around your vibrator, spice things up a little. Oh, and if you don't have a vibrator, they carry them at all the big name drug stores."

Without waiting for Bailey to respond, Tristin grabbed Brent's hand and they sauntered off, leaving Bailey huffing and puffing like the big bad wolf.

"You need to be careful with her," Brent warned. "She loves making life hell for people."

"I'm not the kind of girl who plays nice with someone like that. Whatever she can dish out, I will throw right back at her."

The girl he'd know took no prisoners either and he was glad to see the woman was the same. It was just one of the countless things he had loved about her that summer.

When they got in the truck, Tristin slid over to the middle, sidling right up to him and forcing Brent to work extra hard — yeah, hard wasn't the problem — to keep the truck on the road. "I don't mean to pry or judge, but what exactly did you see in that woman?"

Too many people had asked him that question and Brent didn't have a good answer. "I was lonely and she was there. She was pretty great in the beginning,"

"Despite making you wait for sex," Tristin laughed.

"She's not as innocent as she makes herself sound," Brent replied, because they'd done plenty and he had liked Bailey enough that it kept his interest. Besides, they didn't have the kind of chemistry he shared with Tristin, so waiting wasn't much of a hardship.

"Why did things end between you two?" Tristin asked.

"She wanted more than I could give," he stated, the story of his life. "After a few months, she wanted to move in with me, even pushed to get married. I thought that's what I wanted, but I realized it wasn't with her." With Bailey he was comfortable, but he wasn't happy. He'd never been happy with anyone, except Tristin. "Can we not talk about Bailey?"

She chuckled, her hand drawing the infinity symbol on his thigh and making him crazy. "We can talk about whatever you want," she said.

"I can't talk about anything with your finger doing that," he admitted.

"I can stop—"

"No, don't stop. I love your hands on me."

With that, her hand went higher, but not quite high enough, which was fine since he needed to keep the truck on the road. Every hair on his body stood on end, little fire ants standing up and begging for more.

When they reached his house, he cut the engine and pulled Tristin onto his lap. She went easily, her eyes flickering with the same need he was trying to keep on a leash. She bit the corner of her lip, pushing her hips against his raging hard-on.

"I can't get enough of you," he said.

"I'm all yours," she said, and while Brent wanted to believe that, his cynical side reminded him it was temporary. Yes, she was his now, but in a couple months she'd be on her way, once again leaving him in the dust to nurse his shattered heart.

"I want you in bed," Brent muttered. Last night out by the woodshed was amazing, as was the quickie in the truck, but there was so much of her he wanted to explore, to drive her wild slowly, bringing them both to the edge before pulling back and making it last.

"Then take me to bed," she said.

They got out of the truck and grabbed the bags, but Tristin's seductive little smile invited him to press her against the truck and take a taste.

"Oh for the love of..." Courtney groaned, the front door slamming behind her. "Get a room."

"We were about to," Brent muttered over his shoulder.

"Yeah, well, Cat is here and she needs to talk to Tristin."

What was with people constantly wanting to talk to one or the other of them? Brent was ready to rent a remote cabin in the woods somewhere, more remote than his, and not tell anyone where they were going so they couldn't be walked in on and interrupted again.

"We can pick this back up later," Tristin whispered, amusement in her eyes.

Brent failed to see the humor, but he was nursing a painful erection. He might need a cold shower before he could fire up the grill.

They made their way into the house, finding Cat and Cyn chatting it up at the kitchen table. Lots of female squealing echoed throughout the kitchen as Tristin and Cat said their hellos, it's been so long, great to see ya's. Brent tried not to feel bitter about everyone stealing time from them. Tristin had been friends with everyone the summer she'd spent in Lilac Ridge. Of course people would be happy to see her again.

"How was the hike?" Cyn asked when the conversation settled down and Tristin took a seat at the table with her friends.

"Fantastic," Tristin responded, winking at Brent as he put the groceries away. He couldn't disagree. He'd enjoyed the hike, but the time in the water and then in the truck made it the best hike ever.

"So what's up?" Tristin asked. He hoped she was as eager he to get through this and send Cat on her merry way so things could venture into the bedroom.

"I'm the events coordinator and marketing director for the parks and recreation department here in town. We run a summer hiking camp and have a nurse on staff to keep insurance down. Our nurse is pregnant and was just put on limited duty, so she can't go on the hikes. We have a camp this week, so you can imagine the predicament I'm in."

"Are you asking me to be the nurse?" Tristin asked.

"I know it's short notice and this is your summer vacation, but you were so outgoing when you were here all those years ago and you just went on a hike today so you must still love it and you're a nurse and—"

"Okay, Cat, breathe," Tristin encouraged. "I'd love to help."

"Oh, God! Thank you! I owe you big time!"

Brent didn't know a lot about the summer camps except that they existed. He was curious to find out how much this would take Tristin away, but there was way too much estrogen in his kitchen and he had to get the grill fired up.

Besides, he didn't want to be the jealous dick who told her not to go. Their time was limited, according to her, so why in hell would she agree to this when it didn't involved him?

"I'll be outside," he muttered, but none of the women seemed to notice him leaving. When he reached the grill, Rascal skittered out of the woods, chirping at him.

He got into the locked bin where he kept a tub of dog food for the critter and grabbed a handful, holding out his palm. She came right over, standing on her hind legs as she took one nugget at a time and nibbled. "At least I have you," he sighed, but even though he loved the little raccoon, she wasn't going to be able to patch up the big hole in his heart that Tristin was going to leave at the end of the summer.

That's why he had to convince her to stay.

# Chapter 7

"YOU JUST GOT here and you're leaving already," Brent whined. If he wasn't so damn sexy, it might annoy her, but instead Tristin focused on how she could make it up to him.

"Cat isn't going to be able to find someone else on such short notice," Tristin defended. She couldn't just leave Cat and all those campers hanging.

"She's pretty resourceful, I'm sure she could find someone."

"Yes, resourceful, that's why she asked me. I'm qualified and available. Problem solved."

He continued to feed his little raccoon friend, pouting like a little boy. She came up behind him, rubbing his shoulders, then kissing his neck, her fingers trailing across the tattoos that peeked out from his sleeves. "You were going to take me to bed," she reminded him.

He just grunted.

"What? I'm going camping for a week and suddenly you don't want me?"

He tossed the rest of the kibble on the ground and stood from the log he'd perched on, facing Tristin. Even upset, he took her breath away. She wanted to kiss away all the disappointment, remind him of the explosive connection they shared.

"I didn't dedicate that song so I could get laid," he said. "I want you, every part of you, but it doesn't seem like you want the same thing."

When she'd heard that dedication, her instincts told her to ignore it, stay away, because she couldn't give him what he wanted. Cyn, however, insisted, appealing to Tristin's nurturing nature that at the very least, she had to give him some closure. She knew it was a bad idea to come here, but couldn't deny her own curiosity or desire.

"I told you I'm only here for the summer," she reminded him. She didn't want to feed any illusions he might have about a future. Tristin wasn't the staying kind. She'd tried that once and the result had gutted her.

"Even less than that now that you'll be gone hiking every other week."

"I don't want to fight," she said, deciding it was best to let him work through this on his own rather than talk in circles. "I have to go get my gear together and pack."

"So you're skipping out on dinner?" he growled.

His temper should raise her hackles, but Brent had always been the brooding kind. As a young man, he'd snap to her defense in a heartbeat, fighting over her and for her. It had been a huge turn on, as had the fights they'd had on occasion, usually because she'd made plans without him. He was possessive, demanding back then, but she'd loved him enough it didn't bother her.

Even now, it didn't bother her except to know how much she was going to hurt him. She couldn't, however, just ignore it and let it slide. "I'm not going to have dinner with you if you're going to pout the whole time."

"I'm not pouting," he grumbled. "I just want to spend time

with you. As much as possible."

"That's what I want too, but I'm not going to let down a friend who needs my help. I promise to make it up to you," and while she thought sex was a great way to do that, there were so many other things they could do together. "Let's go fishing next weekend."

When he nodded, she stepped up to him, resting her hands on his strong arms. "Everyone left, so if you want to go upstairs while we wait for the coals…"

One corner of his mouth lifted with the faintest smirk. "You have a one-track mind."

"There's more than one track, but they all lead us to the same destination."

~ ♥ ~

Brent didn't mind a little hard work, but two straight eighteen-hour days took their toll. And he still wasn't finished.

He'd ordered special materials for the sign Maddie commissioned for the equine assisted therapy center. Brent knew the sign was important to her, so he'd taken extra care with it, but because delivery of the materials had been delayed, the sign was now cutting into his time with Tristin.

The weeks were passing by too quickly. That first week she'd spent hiking with the campers had been pure hell, but the time they'd spent when she returned made it seem like she'd never been away, not for that week, and not for the past ten years. She was on her second week as the camp nurse, but that also meant they had six weeks left before she headed for Wyoming.

All of his subtle attempts to get her to change her mind about leaving had failed. It was time to up his game, starting tonight when she returned. First, he had to finish this sign.

"Need some help?" Darren asked.

"Would love some," Brent said.

"Really?" Darren asked. Since Brent preferred to do things on his own, he usually turned down Darren's help, but he had to get the sign up before he could see Tristin.

"Yeah, the posts are set, so we can mount the sign." It'd be easier with two people anyway, even though he'd figured out tricks of the trade to finish a two-person job with just one set of arms.

"All right. Show me what to do."

Darren was smart, a quick study, and damned handy with a power drill. Brent showed him where to drill the holes for the brackets and Darren got to work. When Maddie popped over with two glasses of iced tea, he wanted to keep working, but Darren seemed content to stop and steal a kiss from his soon-to-be wife before enjoying the cold drink, so Brent took a break too.

"This is beautiful," Maddie said, studying the sign that leaned against his truck. "You are so talented."

Brent had worked with her to sketch out the design, but the sketches didn't do justice to the finished product. The special molding he'd ordered was the perfect embellishment. Brent had painted two horseshoes, one facing up and the other facing down, interlocking with each other. It was the logo for The Lucky Horseshoe, the name she'd decided on for the therapy center. "Hopefully business will pick up once the sign is up."

"You've been open a week, and you had more clients here than in your office," Darren laughed. "If business picks up much more, I'll have to start scaring your clients away so I can have time with my wife."

"I'm not your wife yet," she responded.

"And not soon enough, either," he said, pulling her against him.

Brent took a long drink and looked away, trying not to think about how much he wanted to do the same thing with Tristin...and so much more.

"Think we can finish this up?" Brent asked the happy

couple.

"Tristin coming back today?" Maddie asked.

He nodded.

"Good, that means you won't keep Darren too long. I'll leave you boys to it."

She kissed her man one more time and sauntered off with a bounce in her step.

"I'm a damn lucky man," Darren said, watching her until she disappeared inside the barn. "How are things with Tristin?"

"Good, I think. Haven't convinced her to stay, though."

"Give it time," Darren encouraged, but time was the one thing they didn't have. She insisted she was only here for the summer and it was his busiest time of year. He couldn't ignore work even if he wanted to. Customers depended on him, as did Courtney. He needed to earn money, needed to keep his customers happy and coming back.

Tristin had been a huge help. She attended fairs and trade shows with him, charming potential clients and earning him new leads. His sales so far this summer had been higher than ever, so either the economy really had bounced back or people couldn't say no to Tristin.

"Let's get the sign up," Brent said. With the brackets in place and the two of them hefting the big sign, it slid into position with perfect precision.

The only thing left to do was put the screws through the posts to secure the sign.

"I can finish this if you want to take off," Darren offered.

He trusted Darren to do a good job, after all, he was one-third owner of the therapy center, but Brent had been paid to do a job and he would finish it. "I'm all set here. Why don't you head back to your woman," Brent suggested.

"Don't have to tell me twice," Darren said.

Brent secured the screws, two on each side, and put his gear away, keeping it at the speed limit as he headed through town.

He had hoped for a text from Tristin when she returned but figured she was catching up with Cyn. Between Courtney and Cat, Cyn wasn't around much. She had also picked up some administrative work at the hospital to keep busy since she couldn't do much while in a cast. Because Tristin spent most of her time when she wasn't camping with him, he didn't want to act like a jealous dick if Tristin was spending time with her friend. He planned to grab a shower and hit the RV, maybe entice her out to dinner before they returned to his place for dessert.

Courtney's car was gone when he pulled up to the house. Maybe he'd rethink dinner out if Tristin was around. Stinking of lumber and sweat, Brent kicked out of his work boots and headed upstairs. The smell of vanilla raised his hackles and slowed his steps. He came to an abrupt stop when he found a naked woman in his bed.

"Bailey, what the hell?"

The vanilla should have tipped him off. She'd always claimed it was a natural aphrodisiac and insisted on burning candles whenever they had sex.

"Rumor has it your radio girl skipped town. I thought you might want some comforting."

"Get dressed and get out," he demanded. He always tried to be nice to Bailey because he'd hurt her, but now she'd crossed a line.

How the hell did she get in his house? Okay, granted, he never locked the door, but never needed to. Bailey lived in town. It was a hike to walk out to his place. Unless she'd hidden her car.

He hoofed it downstairs and out the front door, unsure what to do. The decision was made when Tristin padded down the path from her RV. When the bright smile faded, he knew Bailey had made her appearance behind him.

"I just got home and she was here," he said. "Uninvited and unwanted." It was cruel, but Tristin was the only one who mattered. If he hurt Bailey now, it would be her own doing.

Tristin had no reason to trust him, but she also had no reason not to. When he was nineteen, he'd been committed to her that summer. He'd never cheated on anyone, not then and not now, and as far as he was concerned, he and Tristin were together, so there was no room in his life for another woman.

Even if there was, it wouldn't be Bailey.

Brent stepped toward Tristin, who remained still on the lawn just this side of the path. "I was going to grab a shower and come find you," he said, stopping in front of her.

Her smile returned. "I just got back too. I'm desperate for a shower. Maybe we should share the water."

"You do know I'm standing right here," Bailey said.

"And Brent said you were uninvited and unwanted. That was your queue to leave," Tristin responded.

God, he loved her feisty attitude. She stripped out of her shirt, not concerned at all with Bailey as an audience. "See how dirty I am," she said, then bit down on her lower lip.

Brent followed her lead, tugging his shirt over his head and tossing it on the ground next to hers. "Not as dirty as I am."

He was pretty sure she purred then. The sound shot a thrill straight to his groin. Yeah, Bailey needed to make an exit now or she was going to have a show.

"Unbelievable," Bailey muttered, tapping on her phone as she stomped up the driveway.

"I have to start locking the doors," Brent said.

"Forget her. How about that shower?"

Tristin had been thinking about a shower for the last three days. A shower with Brent was just the icing on the very fine cake.

She didn't mind camping, but owned an RV because she preferred the modern conveniences of a bed and shower. Four nights in the wilderness would have been fine under normal circumstances, but this week's campers were comprised of horny teenagers who went to great lengths to sneak out of their tents and meet up for make-out sessions in the woods.

Ten year olds were much easier to deal with.

She was exhausted and ready for a long sleep, but with Brent half naked already, she decided she could sleep when she was dead, or at least when she got to Wyoming.

"You're not mad about Bailey?" Brent asked as they stood on his lawn, just taking each other in as if it had been longer than five days.

"You didn't invite her here and you didn't do anything with her, right?" she asked. She had no claim to Brent, but she didn't tend to sleep with guys who were involved with someone else, and she was here because of the man gripping her waist, so she'd be more than pissed if he had fallen into bed with his ex.

"I didn't, I wouldn't. You're all I can think about."

"Then I have no reason to be mad. Let's forget about her."

"She was naked in my bed, so we're going to have to change the linens."

The woman was a total lunatic. How she could go from saying she'd made Brent wait two months to showing up naked in his bed, uninvited, no less, boggled Tristin. One thing was clear, Bailey needed therapy. As for the sheets, "Maybe we should burn them."

"Shower first. Sheet-burning later."

She squealed when he picked her up and flung her over his shoulder. "You're such a cave man," she laughed.

He put her down in the bathroom. "Get started without me, I'll take care of the bed."

Tristin followed his orders, stripping down and stepping into the shower. The warm spray was almost better than an orgasm. Almost.

It didn't take long for Brent to join her, in all his naked glory. The man was amazing, perfect and beautiful and she wanted to touch every inch of him.

"You look like you have ideas," he drawled. "Please tell me you have ideas."

"Oh, I have ideas." She grabbed the soap and ran it over his chest, shoulders, arms, putting it back in the dish so she could use both hands to lather him up.

When the lather was thick, her hands drifted south where he was already hot and hard. Brent groaned as she gripped him, her hand sliding up and down with slow, firm strokes. "I love your ideas," he said, his head back, eyes closed. Her veins thrummed with the power to make him moan with such pleasure.

But she wanted to do more, so she let the water wash the soap away. Still stroking him, she kissed his chest, her tongue playing with one nipple ring, then the other, eliciting a string of pleasured curses that encourage her on. She kissed him, down, down, down, until she was kneeling before him, his hands tangled in her hair.

She traced the pattern of the infinity tattoo below his belly button, loving that he still had it and hadn't had it covered with other designs. She wondered how many other women had done this to him, but pushed the thought aside. She never let another man touch hers; maybe Brent had protected his in the same way.

When her mouth covered him, he swore again, his hands tightening and sending one hell of a zinger south. It had been like this when they were teenagers too, Brent demanding yet gentle, Tristin eager to please him.

Her heart pounded wildly, matching the rhythm she found he liked. She ached to have him touch her, to make her writhe with the same wild passion, but she redirected the need to focus on him, the way his hips moved, the way his fingers clung to her, the sounds he made.

"Tris," he whispered, in pleasure, in warning, but she wanted to take him all the way, to show him how much he meant to her, even if they did only have a few more weeks.

When he came, it was a powerful high, one she hadn't felt in a decade, and one that could fuel an addiction. She stayed with him, kissing and caressing his sensitive skin through every last jerk of his hips. When he released her hair, she kissed the intricate pattern of ink on his left thigh.

"You're making me crazy," he murmured.

"Yeah? I like you crazy," she said, getting her feet under her and thankful for the yoga that kept her muscles limber.

She stopped to play with his nipple rings, her tongue, her fingers reveling in his continued groans. "I got those to remind me to stay the course. Never used them for pleasure before you."

"I love them," she said. Some people couldn't pull off piercings or tattoos, but Brent wore both like a God and she wanted to worship him.

"I love that you love them. God, that feels good."

She switched sides, her tongue tracing across his chest until she found the other ring. "I'd be selfish to let you do that to me all night," he said, reaching behind her. When his arm returned, he eased the soap across her back. "Time to have my wicked way with you."

She liked the sound of that, reveling in the tantalizing caress of his hands. He washed her very thoroughly, taking more time than he needed to in certain special areas before washing her hair. Every second revved her up, but he only teased, not even bringing her to the edge. When the water cut off, she wanted to ask what the hell, but the look in his eyes told her everything. He had plans, delicious plans.

They didn't even dry off. He kissed the hell out of her, backing her into his bedroom and onto a lush blanket on the bed.

"My turn for a taste," he said, his gaze washing over her with intent that had her writhing from just the promise of his touch. Brent had been the first boy to ever go down on her and he'd been good at it all those years ago. She'd found out firsthand that now, as a man, not a boy, he was a God when it came to using his tongue. She wanted to beg him to stop looking and get on with it, but the anticipation amped up her desire. "But where to start?"

"Anywhere," she breathed, the ache between her legs screaming *here, right here!*

He groaned, kneeling next to the bed and tugging her to him. "Right here, I think," and he kissed just above her knee, his tongue leaving a delicious trail up the inside of her thigh. Then he skipped over to the other one, teasing the same trail before using his finger to trace the infinity tattoo below her belly button.

"I love this," he said, his lips covering the pattern.

"I love your mouth on it," she whispered, but where she really wanted his mouth was just a little further south. "Are you going to torment me forever?"

"Forever is exactly what I had in mind," he said, but before she could remind him this was only temporary, his mouth was where she needed it to be, his tongue sweeping up her center and making every logical thought in her head go on vacation.

"Holy mother," she cried out, her hips jerking up, begging for more. Brent placed two firm hands on her hips to hold her down and further torment her, all the while using his magical caress to drive her to the edge.

No one had ever touched her like this, no one, and God, she wanted it to last…forever.

But forever was just a story written by people who had never lost anything, anyone. Forever didn't actually exist.

His tongue swept away those rogue thoughts, reminding her that here and now was how she lived, how she survived. When he groaned against her delicate flesh, his stubble scraping as his tongue caressed, she whispered his name, or maybe moaned…a plea for more, to hurry and lift her up to that place only he could take her.

And he did, taking her higher than she'd ever been. Tristin floated, the brilliant white of pleasure blinding her, her cries so high-pitched they threatened to shatter the windows. Floating,

floating, up, and back down until the white faded and she opened her eyes to find Brent hovering over her, the need so potent in his eyes that she was desperate to float away with him again.

When he pushed inside her, slow and strong, she knew that's where they were destined to go.

# Chapter 8

WHEN TRISTIN OFFERED to lend a hand for Spay and Taco Tuesday, she thought it'd be a breeze. She may not deal with animals on a regular basis, but she was a nurse, so figured the basics would come into play.

She never even got a chance to exercise the basics. Her job wasn't to assist with the medical care, but to herd cats.

Literally.

One of the volunteers at Jill Hale's animal rescue had forgotten to latch the cages that house the overabundance of felines. Now cats were everywhere and it was up to Tristin to get them into their rightful rooms in what Jill preferred to call the pet hotel.

"Come on, baby, let's get you settled," she said to the pretty but skittish gray tabby ready to bolt from her arms.

"I've got one," Cyn yelled, appearing at the end of the aisle, a single crutch lodged in her armpit, the cat hooked in the other arm.

The little tabby bolted out of Tristin's arms, using her head as a climbing pole.

She uttered a string of curses and reached up to extract the cat from her head, her hair tangled in the little fella's claws.

"Oh, God, I'm sorry. Did I startle it?"

"Figure out where that one goes and help me with this," Tristin directed because it was clear she couldn't get out of this mess on her own. Her arms got a workout as she held the cat over her head, the poor thing screeching the whole time. When Cyn reappeared, she hobbled down the aisle. Once she reached Tristin, she leaned on the crutch, her hands circling the cat's torso just below Tristin's.

"We need another set of hands," Cyn said. "Your hair is everywhere."

They moved with little grace to the end of the aisle and called for help when they reached the door. Courtney, who was manning the front desk, came through the door, her eyes widening with amusement. "What happened?"

"He mistook me for a tree," Tristin said. It wasn't the poor guy's fault. He was already a bit freaked out by his short adventure into freedom. Cyn's squeal would have set even the most mellow of felines into a tailspin.

"Okay, sorry if I pull, but he sure did get tangled up here."

It happened so fast, and her hair was so fine, she wasn't sure how he'd gotten into such a knotted mess. With Tristin standing still as a statue, Cyn holding the yowling cat and giggling, and Courtney extricating her hair strand by strand — and also giggling — she was finally freed.

The collective gasps when she pushed her hair from her face had her standing still again.

"Shit. We need to take care of that," Cyn said.

"Take care of what?" Tristin asked. Courtney dug her phone out of her pocket and put the camera on with the screen facing Tristin so it acted like a mirror.

"Oh," and just as she noticed the scratches down her face, the sting of them kicked in.

"Here," Cyn said to Courtney, handing her the little cat.

"Where's your first aid kit?"

"Behind the reception desk. You can't miss it."

Cyn grabbed Tristin's hand and led her to the front, releasing her hand only to grab the first aid kit. She stuffed in down her shirt and grabbed Tristin's hand again. Hand in hand again, Cyn led her to the bathroom and cracked open the case.

"Standard kit. We need to get them some upgraded stuff, and hey, look at that, it's expired."

"People don't think about First Aid kits until they need one," Tristin reminded her.

"I'm upgrading them. This is going to have to do for now."

Tristin wasn't worried. Cleaning the scratches should do the job and prevent infection, especially since they didn't waste any time in taking care of it. Plus, she had a kick ass immune system and took her daily vitamins. She shouldn't be at risk for infection.

"Okay, I'm good. You can stop fussing," Tristin said after Cyn applied the antiseptic ointment.

"Nurses make the worst patients," Cyn mumbled.

"You would know," Tristin retorted since Cyn was the worst of patients.

Undeterred by her injuries, Tristin got back to herding cats. When all the meows were secure, she headed out front to see what else she could help with.

"Slow night," Courtney said. "We're calling it. Maddie and Jill are at the farmhouse getting the food ready."

Because this was their first time, Cyn and Tristin were exempt from bringing food, but still responsible for their own drinks.

They cleaned up and walked across the yard to Jill's farmhouse. She didn't live there anymore since she was married to Austin Hale and lived in his house, but the group had decided it was the perfect location for the Taco part of Spay and Taco Tuesday. The spay part was the clinic that Jill held where pet owners in need could bring their pets to have them spayed or neutered at no cost. Clarissa performed all the surgeries and after, they ate and drank.

"When are you able to do yoga with us again?" Cat asked Courtney when they walked into the kitchen.

"I hate yoga," Courtney said. "Um, I mean, yoga, yay!"

Jill snorted. "I prefer sex as my method of cardio."

Cat and Clarissa snorted this time before Cat said, "Here we go. Between Miss Newly Wed and Miss About to Be Wed, you're making the rest of us jealous."

"Darren and I are abstaining until the wedding," Maddie said, peeling the foil from what looked like a tasty layered dip.

"Wow, really? That's…" Cat said, but Maddie busted out laughing.

"Are you kidding me? I can't even believe I was able to say the word abstain. You are so gullible."

"Shut up. Lots of people do that before they get married," Cat defended.

"Not this girl. Darren is way too hot. I can barely go an afternoon."

A collective sigh filled the room. "Austin and I did it in the loft yesterday," Jill said.

Another collective sigh.

Tristin opened her mouth, but met the glaring scowl of Courtney. "Don't even," she warned.

Right, because nobody wanted to hear about their brother's sex life, or what a God he was in bed.

"I wasn't going to…"

"How many times have I walked in on the two of you? You'd think you'd never heard of a bed or at least a locked door."

Everyone else laughed, but Courtney just shook her head.

"Can we get back to yoga?" Cat suggested. "Your eye surgery was over a month ago now. You should be able to exercise, right? So yoga, because you can't use the *my glasses slide off my face* excuse anymore."

"I've doubled-up on my course load so I can finish school in December instead of dragging it out. I don't have time for yoga."

"Excuses, excuses," Cat murmured. "What about you ladies? Do you do yoga?"

"I'd love to," Tristin said. She often did yoga on her own, but doing a class with someone she liked would be fun.

"Not me," Cyn said.

"You can do yoga with a cast on," Cat interrupted.

Cyn just shook her head. "When this cast is off, I'll bike twenty miles, but I don't want to get twisted up like a pretzel. Well, unless there is a hot guy and an orgasm is involved."

One more collective sigh.

They dug into the food, which included everything from a lemon meringue pie (which Clarissa referred to as a fruit tray), Maddie's seven layer taco dip (which was the only thing taco related), Jill's broccoli salad, and Cat's fruit kebabs. There was an agreement in place to avoid all things pasta since Maddie wanted to fit into her wedding dress in a few weeks.

"So tell me about Sean Beckett," Cyn said.

Not a sigh this time, but a groan. "Don't let his good looks and charm fool you," Cat warned. "He's a womanizer."

"He's the perfect guy for a good time, but not anything long term," Clarissa added.

Maddie, Jill, and Cat all raised their brows at her. "What? I didn't sleep with him. You wouldn't believe what some of my clients talk about when I'm treating their pets."

Then they turned to Maddie. "I can't say anything. As a psychotherapist, I'm committed to privacy and confidentiality."

"That means he's the subject of angst for at least one client," Clarissa added. "Otherwise, she would have said she hadn't heard anything."

"Maybe I'm trying a new tactic, being more mysterious," Maddie said.

"All right, Sean's out. Who is hot, single, and looking for love?" Cyn asked.

"And doesn't own a cat," Cat added, "because I'd like to

find love too."

"You don't like cats?" Tristin asked.

"I love cats," she said.

"But her boyfriends keep ditching the cats with her," Jill added. "I swear half the adoption drives we've done this past year have been to rescue her."

"Shut up. I don't date that much."

Everyone raised their brows again, this time looking at Cat.

"Okay, yeah, I've pretty much expended Lilac Ridge's available population. I need to move."

"Why are you looking for love anyway?" Tristin asked. "September will be here before we know it."

"You guys should stay," Maddie said. "I mean, if things are going well with Brent, why would you want to leave?"

"We're not really the type of gals who stay in one place," Tristin replied.

"Speak for yourself," Cyn said. "I like this town. I wouldn't object to staying."

Cheers all around, except from Courtney, who seemed to be scowling at Tristin. "Brent knows it's only the summer," Tristin said. "He just needs to get me out of his system. I'm sure the perfect woman is out there somewhere."

It hurt to think about Brent with another woman, but Tristin couldn't offer him what he wanted. His roots were here and she didn't have roots.

"I wish a guy would dedicate a song to me on the radio," Cat sighed.

Conversation went back to all of the eligible bachelors in Lilac Ridge and even some in neighboring Sunset Valley. Tristin ate her fill and drank her fill too since Courtney was the designated driver and Jill made a mean margarita. All the talk about men had her missing Brent and wishing his sister was ready to hit the road so Tristin could show him what parts she had missed the most. She liked being here though, with this group of women who had invited her and Cyn into their inner circle with open arms. They didn't always forge these kinds of friendships because they didn't stay in one place long enough.

~ ♥ ~

Peace.

That's why Tristin took a couple months off in the summer. She loved all the seasons, the beautiful autumn colors and milder temperatures, the brisk temps and adrenaline that came with skiing, the rebirth spring offered, but the heat of summer, the calmness of a mountain lake, it helped her find that inner peace she often struggled to keep ahold of.

She'd taken up kayaking a few years ago because it was on her bucket list. First time out, she was addicted. Nothing offered serenity like a sunny day on the water.

"What do you think about skipping out on Wyoming and staying here instead?" Cyn sked, her voice a little too innocent.

"What did you do now?" Tristin demanded. Since this was the second time she'd mentioned it, Tristin suspected Cyn had already taken action toward it.

"I haven't done anything, but you know, I picked up some per diem shifts at the hospital. It's a great place and they are desperate for nurses right now. Aren't you tired of moving every few months?"

Tristin shook her head. "I'm not. You know I don't like staying anywhere very long."

"I think it's the nature of your upbringing. Have you ever tried sticking around someplace?"

Cyn already knew the answer, so Tristin didn't bother to repeat it.

"What's this about?" she asked.

Shrugging was a way to play up the innocence of the whole conversation, but Cyn wouldn't have brought it up if she didn't already have an agenda. "I just thought, well, things are going well with Bear, right?"

It made her chuckle that everyone except Courtney called him Bear. She had definitely noticed how he came across as gruff, but with her, he was sweet and gentle. "Sure, but that's because we both know it's only the summer. I don't think either one of us could handle the pressure of permanent."

"You're so full of shit. You can handle anything."

Cyn gave her credit where it wasn't due. Every time Tristin had a shot of something permanent, she high-tailed it out the relationship faster than a tornado destroyed a mid-west town. It was a fault Tristin was well aware of but had no desire to fix. "I don't have a great track record, remember?"

"Mark and Jesse don't count. You were under duress. You had every right to walk away from both of them."

Except Tristin didn't walk. She abandoned both men at the altar and ran away as fast as she could.

"It's been forever. You need to forgive yourself, not that there's anything to forgive."

She had forgiven herself for not marrying them, because that was the right decision, but the way she'd gone about ending the relationships, well, that was one thing — two, really — she couldn't forgive herself for.

At least Jesse had thanked her. The next morning, he tracked her down at the airport, said she'd been right to call off the wedding, that they'd both regret it. Mark, though, she'd never even given him the chance.

"Did you meet someone?" Tristin asked, putting this back on Cyn and not on her sordid past.

"No, and I'm never going to if we keep moving. Listen, I'm with you. If you're game for Wyoming, so am I, but I just want you to know I'm ready to find something permanent. I'd love for us to do that together."

Tristin couldn't imagine being anywhere without Cyn. They'd met on that plane out of Vegas. It was the cheapest flight she could get that day, heading to Salt Lake City. Tristin was convinced she could find work there. She was a nurse, after all. She should be able to find work anywhere. Cyn had just finished four months at a hospital in Las Vegas, on her way to her next assignment. The idea of moving every few months appealed to Tristin, so she'd picked Cyn's brain for details and Cyn connected her with the agency they still worked with.

After a couple years of jetting from place to place, Tristin proposed the RV and they'd been living on the road ever since.

It had been great, but Tristin wasn't ready for it to end. She had a list of places she wanted to see and experience. She needed to stay on the move so the ghosts couldn't catch up with her.

# Chapter 9

BRENT COULDN'T WIPE the smile off his face. Even as he found Courtney scowling at the kitchen table, stabbing her grapefruit in angst, he didn't care if she made fun of him. He was happy. Happy. It was a first, at least since that summer he'd spent with Tristin. Even that summer didn't compare to the way she made his heart beat now. The biggest difference though, now they had a chance at a future, something neither of them had thought about when they were teenagers. He just had to convince her not to go to Wyoming in September.

"I'm moving out," Courtney declared when Brent grabbed the pot of coffee.

"What?" he asked, stunned. He released the pot and turned to his sister. "No, Court, I'm sorry, we'll try to..." Try to what? Keep it down? Slow it down? Keep it in their pants? He couldn't, didn't want to. Making Tristin writhe and pant and cry his name, it had become all he could think about. That and the future he wanted with her.

"This isn't about you and Tristin, though I have to say, I

won't miss all the noise or exposes."

"Then what?"

"Jill offered me the farmhouse. The new foundation is finished. She wants someone she can trust in the house and I need to be out on my own."

"You're not happy here?" he asked. She had moved in with him a couple years ago. Once discharged from the air force after six years, she'd spent a summer in Europe before traveling by train around the United States. When she started school, though, she'd landed at Brent's at his insistence. She was driven and he didn't want her to worry about bills. Plus, he was lonely and he'd missed his sister.

"Don't get me wrong, I appreciate you taking me in, but I'll be done with school in December and plan to get a life, maybe even a man. I don't want to be bringing him home to my brother's house and risk him getting the shit beat out of him."

"Court," he sighed, "I'm not going to apologize for protecting you." She was only sixteen when that son of a bitch boss of hers took advantage. The guy was twenty-one, but Brent had him on size and fury. Of course, beating the crap out of the bastard got Courtney and their mom fired from the seedy bar, and got Brent a one-way ticket to Uncle Ray's in Lilac Ridge. "And I don't want you to leave."

"It's only four miles down the road," she sighed.

Only four miles, but he wouldn't see her every day, have breakfast with her every morning, watch Arrow with her every Wednesday night, even during the off-season.

He had missed his sister after he got the boot by their parents and hated leaving her to raise herself. He didn't regret protecting her though, nor moving to Lilac Ridge. He'd met Tristin a few months later and made the peaceful little town his home.

Because he'd been forced to abandon Courtney, he wanted to take care of her now, give her whatever he could. He couldn't make up for what she'd missed out on as a kid.

They'd both been forced to grow up too fast, but he could make life easy for her now.

"Oh my God, you're really upset about this," she said. "See, I tell everyone you're just a big teddy bear. How come I'm the only one who gets to see this side of you? You need to make a public show to give me some street cred."

He chuckled at that. "Street cred? Jesus, Tweety-Bird, you run circles around everyone with everything you take on. You've got street cred."

"Yeah, well let's hope that street cred lands me a job. And don't call me Tweety-Bird."

He ignored that last bit and focused on the job thing. "You're quitting too?"

What the hell! It's like his world had been flipped upside down. Tristin walks back into his life and everything is great, but then his sister decides to bail.

"I will be done with my bachelor's degree in six months," she repeated, this time speaking like a robot to get her point across. "You don't need a full-time receptionist slash marketing person and I want to do something that challenges me."

"Most people would love a job as easy as yours."

"Except when they have to field date and hate calls. Oh, and let's not forget all the sex I keep walking in on. You'll be happy when I'm gone, not so many interruptions on the bow-chicka-bow-bow and maybe I won't go blind."

"You traumatized me with that first. Sixteen, for crying out loud."

"And when did you start having sex? Huh? I know Jasmine Wheeler gave you blow-job behind Tully's Quick-Mart when you were fifteen."

"What the? How did?"

"She bragged about it for a month. So gross. She was such a slut. You could have done better."

No arguing that, but working almost full-time at the quick-mart and going to school, Brent thought he deserved to blow off a little steam. Plus, it was Jasmine's idea and he was fifteen, it's not like he made good decisions.

"Can we get back to you leaving?" he sighed.

"I love you and living here has been great, but I need this, so just be happy for me."

All he ever wanted was for Courtney to be happy and safe. She was safe, so all that left was the happy.

Brent hated the thought of letting her go, but she was an adult, not a kid. The woman she'd grown into was fierce, could take care of herself, didn't need her big brother always lurking.

"I love you too, Tweety. If this is what you want, then I'm happy for you."

~ ♥ ~

Cyn had gotten the cast off and they planned to celebrate by tossing back a few drinks for ladies' night, but first, Tristin had promised her friends some outdoor yoga.

Technically, she wasn't certified to teach yoga, but she'd completed the training years ago and practiced the art regularly. Despite providing that disclaimer, her friends had pleaded with her to lead them in a few sessions a week, even the ones who had been reluctant to join a class with Cat.

"You look a little pale," Cyn observed, moving in closer.

"I'm fine," Tristin insisted, pushing Cyn out of her personal space. She was fighting a low-grade fever but thought the fresh air and exercise might help boost her immune system and purge whatever was trying to bring her down.

They had decided to do it at Brent's because it was so quiet and peaceful. Austin had arrived with Jill and Darren had driven Maddie over. Brent decided to take a break from work to ensure a quiet environment, so all three men sat in chairs on the edge of the lawn, watching with interest.

"You three could join us," she offered.

"This is a custom-tailored Italian suit," Austin said, stroking the lapel of his jacket. "It's designed for my ass in a chair, not sticking up in the air."

"Chicken," Jill teased.

Tristin pointed at Darren.

"I'm more of a voyeur," he replied.

"Pervert," Maddie jested.

"I learned from the best, babe. You love to gawk at me at the gym. It's only fair I return the affection."

Tristin shifted her gaze to Brent. "I prefer to observe before I try something new," he said, a playful lilt to his smile. "I'll take a private lesson later."

She'd be happy to give him one too, once her fever broke. Time to focus on the task at hand. "Okay, ladies, I guess it's just us. Anyone have objections to these handsome gentleman observing?"

"Since all eyes will be on either you, Jill, or Maddie, it doesn't bother me," Cat said, "except for the fact I don't have some hot guy gawking at me."

"You have five seconds to start before I find something less exercisey to do with my time," Courtney snarled. "And don't make me do any of those poses that'll make this spandex dive into places unknown."

"Ditto," Cyn added.

"Okay," Tristin started amongst the giggles. "Stand and take a deep breath in while raising arms overhead." Tristin did the action, keeping her eyes open to ensure everyone followed her lead. The fresh air felt good, but Brent's gaze on her made it difficult to concentrate.

"Now, crouch down and place both hands on the mat. Jump or step both feet back into plank position."

Tristin jumped her feet back and almost toppled over. She had to focus, forget Brent was there, despite the heat of his gaze and its effects on her body.

"Lower your body toward the ground and into upward-facing dog. Hold there for several long, deep breaths."

Closing her eyes, she tried to balance through the light-headedness, but it seemed to get worse, not better, as her body temperature spiked. "Okay, let's...press back up into downward-facing dog."

When Tristin got there, she toppled over. She tried to breathe through it, to push the fever out, but it didn't relent.

She felt Brent had her side before he even touched her. "Jesus, Tris, you're burning up."

"I knew something wasn't right. You never get pale, not even in the dead of winter," Cyn said from her other side. "We need to get her to the ER."

Tristin shook her head. "I'm fine."

"Shut. Up. You are not fine. You're on fire. You need to see a doctor."

"I'll go to a walk-in clinic," Tristin conceded. "I don't need the ER."

Brent scooped her up and carried her to his truck. Tristin closed her eyes because the fever and dizziness made it too difficult to keep them open. Everything went black and quiet and when she opened her eyes, she heard the tell-tale signs of being in a hospital. "I said not the ER," she groaned.

"I was driving, I made the call," Brent growled.

"You're sexy when you go all alpha male," she said, "but please stop worrying. I'm sure it's just the flu."

"We'll let the doctors make the diagnosis," he said, one hand brushing the hair from her face.

"How about we blow this pop-stand and go back to your place where you can play doctor and I'll be the obedient patient." That sounded way more fun than being poked and prodded in the ER. Not that she didn't trust her fellow nurses, but Tristin preferred to treat, not be treated.

"We'll do that later. Right now, you're going to play nice with the doctors and nurses so they can get you on the road to recovery."

# Chapter 10

CAT SCRATCH FEVER had Tristin down for a week. She had missed the last hiking camp, but since Cyn was out of her cast, she stepped in. Today was the first day Tristin felt like a human being and she'd been dying to get out of the house.

Brent was still in worry mode, so she promised to take it easy, only going out to do a little shopping.

Now her phone was ringing...again. It was the fifth call from the Washington area code. Tristin hadn't stayed in touch with anyone from college and was picky about who she gave her number to, which was why she'd ignored the first four calls. At this point she felt obligated to give the poor guy or gal a break.

Since she was driving back to Brent's from the grocery store, she hit the bluetooth in her truck. "Hello?"

"Tristin," the voice said.

"This is she."

"It's me, Mark."

Her heart plummeted into her gut, and not in the good way.

She hadn't talked to Mark since their wedding day, despite his efforts to resolve things. First she'd ignored his calls. When that didn't deter him, she'd gone so far as to change her number.

"How did you get my number?" she demanded.

He chuckled. "Not even the courtesy of a 'hi, Mark, how are you?' Not sure why I'm surprised given that you dumped me at the altar."

Leaving him like that without explanation wasn't a shining moment in her past, but it was all she could do to retain a smidgen of self-preservation. She couldn't marry a man she didn't love, a man she resented for having held their daughter when she didn't. While she had convinced herself she'd forgiven him — knowing he'd done the best he could under such grave circumstances — hearing his voice now stirred up all the anger into a funnel cloud that surrounded her and threatened to suck her in.

"Hi,," she sighed, but she couldn't offer any more than that.

"I called your parents, they gave me your number."

She'd been adamant that her parents not give her number out, that if someone wanted to reach her, they call and let her know. Of course, her parents had been more than disappointed in her decision to bail on her wedding day and they adored Mark, so that was two strikes against her.

It had been years, though. Five years since that fateful day. Granted, Tristin hadn't given him any closure, but he had to have moved on by now. While she wanted to demand his reason for calling and get the call over with, she'd hurt him enough to last two lifetimes, so she waited.

"I, uh, I got married."

"That's great. Congratulations." The sentiment sounded hollow despite its authenticity. If she'd known, if they'd stayed in touch or she had some warning he would call, she could have prepared herself, but out of the blue like this, Tristin didn't know how to deal with the tornado of emotions and questions.

"Thanks. That's not why I called."

She waited again, her mind running through countless scenarios for his reason behind the call. Even the worst thing she came up with didn't prepare her for what he eventually said. "We had a baby, a girl."

"Oh," she sighed.

So this was it, his closure, to call her and pour salt on the wound of losing their daughter. He had moved on, gotten over their loss, found love, had a family.

And now, he was throwing it in her face.

"She's sick," he mumbled. "Leukemia."

"Oh, God," she choked out as the past pummeled her. Lights coming at her from her peripheral vision, the impact that robbed her breath, everything going dark, waking up with the pain across her lower belly and that empty feeling she continued to live with, as if a piece of her had been ripped out and buried.

Pulling into the next parking lot she came to, Tristin shut the truck off and tried to breathe. "I'm so sorry," she whispered. They'd already lived through the tragedy of losing a daughter. Tristin knew she wasn't strong enough to survive that twice.

"The doctor wants to do a stem cell transplant. When I told him about Angelica…"

"You want to use her cord blood," she finished, the unspoken request pouring gasoline on her anger. Mark hadn't cared about saving Angelica's cord blood, but Tristin insisted, knowing if the unthinkable happened, the baby's own cord blood would offer the best chance of survival. Tristin had completed the paperwork and paid the annual storage fee every year since. "How do you even know it's a match?"

"It'll have to be tested, but the doctor is hopeful, said the chances are better than from a stranger."

Her eyes stung, but she blinked back the tears. The cord blood wasn't something she thought about except for the one time every year when the charge appeared on her bank statement.

"I can't do this right now," she said.

"Do not hang up on me, Tristin," he demanded. It unsettled her because Mark wasn't the demanding type. He had always been kind, gentle. "I've been calling for three days. My daughter will die."

*Like my daughter did.*

When Mark replied with, "our daughter," Tristin realized she had said it out loud. "You still hate me, don't you?" he added.

Tristin shook her head. She didn't hate him. She never even thought of him. He was part of her past, a part she didn't like to think about.

"I never thought you'd sacrifice an innocent life to get back at me," he murmured.

"I'm not," she defended. "You call me out of the blue and drop all this on me and just expect me to say yes without even thinking about it. You didn't even want to save her cord blood."

"I was twenty-two years old, for chrissake. I was a stupid kid who didn't understand what it could do. Now, I'm a father and have the chance to save my daughter's life, something I failed to do last time."

Mark had held it together. The moment she'd woken up in the hospital, he'd been stoic, telling her about Angelica, trying to help Tristin deal with the grief despite her cruelty. She pushed and pushed and pushed him away, but he clung to an impossible hope that they could survive the tragedy.

"Angelica's death wasn't your fault," she said, the tears pouring now, her breaths ragged as she fought against the building sobs.

"It wasn't yours, either," he said.

Tristin disagreed. There were so many things she could have done differently to change the course of events. She had taken on the extra shift despite how tired she was, and she'd stayed late because the incoming nurse wanted to take her brother to the airport. If Tristin had followed Mark's request and stayed home...

Where would they be now? Married? Divorced? Maybe Angelica would have gotten leukemia and died.

"What do you need from me?" she asked.

"Really?" he asked, the surprise in his voice gutting her. "You'll let us have it?"

"I'm not a monster," she whispered, but Mark had seen her at her worst, endured the grief-stricken anger and resentment directed at him.

"I know this must be difficult—"

"Don't. Do not try to comfort me," she demanded. She had nothing to lose because she had already lost everything, but Mark, the one who had built a new life for himself, once again had everything to lose. "Just tell me what you need me to do." That's how she survived, by focusing on other's needs and nursing them back to health.

Since the blood was registered to her, she had to sign papers to release it. Mark had everything and offered to fax or email it. She recalled seeing a fax in Brent's office, but didn't know the number, so told Mark to email and she'd get it back to him tomorrow.

When the call ended, Tristin was numb. From head to toe, she felt nothing. Medically, her heart still beat in her chest because she still drew breath, felt the pulse when pressing her fingers to her neck, but she was hollow, empty, the way she'd been that day she was supposed to marry Mark.

The way she'd been when about to marry Jesse, too.

Numb. Hollow. Alone.

She looked around to regain her bearings, spotting Madigan's Pub across the street. Instead of starting the truck up and heading to Brent's, Tristin climbed out and locked up, dodging the few cars that passed as she crossed over to the pub. A margarita might jump start her emotions. If not, several would guarantee a hangover. She'd rather be sick than numb.

One guy sat at the bar and a couple booths were occupied, but otherwise the place was ghost city.

Sean was behind the bar. He abandoned the conversation with the man at the other end and came to where Tristin took up residence.

"Here," she said, pushing her keys and cell phone across the bar. "Oh, and this." She pulled a twenty from her pocket. "You guys have a taxi in this town?"

"We have a few Uber drivers," he said.

"Great. Just give all that to the driver when I'm not able to sit upright on this stool anymore. And no matter what I say or how much I threaten you, do not give me the phone."

"Or the keys?"

"I won't ask for the keys."

"Care to make a wager on that?" he chuffed.

She'd only met him a couple times. He didn't know her, didn't know her story, and therefore, didn't know he was making a losing bet. "Absolutely, I'll bet my bar tab. When I win, my drinks are on the house."

"And when I win?" he drawled.

"You won't, so how about a Benjamin?"

"You're on," he declared, extending his hand across the bar. "What can I get you?"

A time machine would be great, but since that was impossible, she'd settle for the next best thing. "Margarita with sugar, extra strong and super-size me," she demanded.

"Coming right up."

A couple minutes later, she slurped down half the drink.

"Might want to slow down," Sean advised.

"Life is too short to take it slow." That's why she took another long drink.

He chuckled and grabbed her gear from the bar, stuffing the keys in his front pocket and the phone in his back pocket. He left the twenty on the bar.

When Sean delivered her third margarita, it was half the size and watered down. Just meant she drank it faster.

"Well, well, well, if it isn't the infamous Tristin May," a female voice chirped from behind her.

Tristin spun on the bar stool, too far, so she used the bar to push her back the other way. "Beatrice," she slurred.

"Bailey," the woman corrected.

"Riiiiight, Bai-ley."

"You're drinking like a woman who's been dumped. I think that's a new record for Bear, two months."

"I didn't get dumped." Not that it mattered. She was a few weeks left in Lilac Ridge. In the end, she was going to hurt Brent, because Bailey had it all wrong. Brent wasn't emotionally unavailable. Tristin was. "What do you want, Bailey?"

"Just the satisfaction of being right. Toodaloo."

More people filed into the pub. When Maddie and Clarissa walked in, they spotted her right away and rushed over.

"You here for ladies night?" Maddie asked, giving her a hug.

"Absolutely," Tristin sang, stumbling off the stool when Maddie pulled away. Tristin made like she intended to slide off and hugged Clarissa too.

She had no idea it was ladies' night, but what the hell, she was there and well on her way.

"Oooh, margarita. I'm having one too. What about you, Riss?"

"I'd love one. Make sure he does sugar and salt," Clarissa responded.

"Awesome. You two grab a table before this place fills up."

"Tell Sean to put it on my tab," Tristin slurred, "and order me another."

She followed Clarissa through the now crowded pub to a table near the front. "There's music tonight. Zack Davis is singing. He's great."

Tristin nodded and smiled, wondering if Zack Davis was someone she should know or someone she recently met.

Nothing came to her, but Clarissa didn't seem concerned, so Tristin stopped with the head bobbing and looked around the pub. She spotted Bailey again, sidled up next to a man who looked like he was eying escape routes.

"What's her story?" Tristin asked, nodding in that direction.

"Bailey?" Clarissa asked. "I have no idea. She moved here a few years ago. Has a big chip on her shoulder, but I'm not privy to where the chip came from. She puts off some seriously bad vibes, so I've kept my distance."

"Bad vibes?" Maddie said, balancing three margaritas between her two hands. "You must be talking about Bailey. I've tried to cleanse her aura, you know, on the sly, but her aura needs a frontal lobotomy."

Tristin took her drink, as did Clarissa. The three of them clanked glasses before taking a long sip. Either Tristin had developed a tolerance, or Sean made her a watered-down version again because there wasn't enough tequila to leave the usual bitter aftertaste. It was still refreshing though, but it had yet to fill the void she was nursing.

When Tristin finished her drink, Clarissa looked at her with a raised brow. "How many of those have you had?"

"I'm not counting," Tristin replied.

"Well, you might want to slow down," Maddie suggested.

"People need to stop saying that to me," Tristin complained. She had one speed and it was full-speed ahead. Anyone who didn't understand that could eat her dust. "I wouldn't drink them so fast if Sean didn't water them down."

"Mine's perfect," Maddie cooed. "Oh, look, the rest of the gang is here."

Tristin turned to find Cyn, Courtney, and Jill Butler-Hale walking toward them. Hellos and hugs went all around and Cyn gave her a questioning gaze, which Tristin ignored.

"I'm going to get a Coke," Courtney said when the hugs were done.

"Can you get me a margarita? I'm running a tab."

"I don't do that," Courtney said and kept on walking.

"It's her background," Jill explained. "She doesn't mind hanging out with us, but she won't get us drinks."

Tristin understood. She knew about Courtney and Brent's parents, of what they'd endured as kids.

"I'd love a margarita," Jill said. "Anyone else besides Tristin?"

"I'd love one, too," Cyn said, but Maddie and Clarissa waved her off.

"Don't tell him the drink is for me. He keeps watering them down," Tristin called after Jill.

Jill gave a salute and headed off.

"So, what's going on?" Cyn asked.

"Nothing."

"Right, you have that look, and you're drunk before midnight. Now spill it."

Not in a million years was she going to talk about that phone call. Tonight was about filling the void in her chest.

"Ooh, I knew something was off when we walked in. Do tell," Maddie encouraged.

"Nothing is off, nothing is going on. I'm enjoying ladies' night, that's all."

"All you've done is slurp and complain about your drinks. That's hardly enjoying," Clarissa pointed.

"Did you and Brent get in a fight?" Cyn prodded.

"No, everything is fine. He's fine. Oh, so fine."

A collective sigh went around the table. "Quick, before Courtney gets back, you have to tell us, how far do his tattoos go?" Maddie asked.

"Aren't you getting married next month?" Tristin asked. The M-word sent a shiver down Tristin's spine.

"Married," Maddie sighed with the whimsical air of a bride-to-be, "but I'm not dead. Darren has a double horseshoe tattoo on his chest. So yummy. But Bear's tattoos go on forever."

That they did. Tristin loved his ink. Every inch meant

something to him. Every night after they made love, Tristin traced along the patterns, encouraging him to tell the story behind the artwork.

"Does he have his, you know, tattooed?" Maddie asked.

"Oh, for Pete's sake. I've never met a therapist who couldn't verbalize the parts of the body," Clarissa jested.

"No, his penis" Tristin emphasized because it was fun to tease Maddie, "has no ink, but he does have tattoos on his upper thighs and hips."

"Oh, please tell me you are not talking about my heathen brother," Courtney whined when she returned with her Coke.

"Maddie ashked," Tristin said, aware of the slur because her tongue had grown three sizes, just like the Grinch's heart.

Maddie shrugged. "I tried to do it while you weren't here, out of reshpect and everything."

Courtney rolled her eyes before glaring at Tristin. "What? Your brother is hot. It would be shellfish if I didn't answer the question."

"I'm allergic to shellfish," Clarissa poked, winking at Tristin.

"Do not make fun of me, I am a shitty week, had, I had a shitty week." Between cat scratch fever and that phone call, she deserved a few margaritas, and not the watered-down variety.

"How much have you had to drink?" Courtney asked, her disapproval palpable, but Tristin wasn't here to impress the doting baby sister.

"Not quite enough," Tristin said, looking for Jill and hoping to hell her next drink was fully loaded.

She wanted to tell Courtney not to judge her, but that would require further explanation, something Tristin wasn't ready to give.

Any additional discussion was interrupted when Jill returned with drinks.

"My new BFF," Tristin joked, taking the drink.

"Me or the drink?" Jill laughed.

"Yes," Tristin responded, taking a long sip. A guy passed by with a guitar, to whom everyone said hello before he set up. In only took him a few minutes to tune his guitar before he introduced himself and started singing.

And of all songs, he started with *Springsteen*.

With a soothing caress, the song eased into her soul, every note pumping like oxygen through her veins. Her chest tightened, heart thumping so hard she could hear it in her ears.

"So romantic," Maddie sighed. "Look at you, all teary eyed just thinking about that dedication."

"Bear is such a sweetheart," Clarissa added.

"I keep telling you all he's a big teddy bear, but no one believes me," Courtney said.

"He is," Tristin said, swiping at the stupid tears.

Angelica was gone. There was nothing that would change that. Giving Mark's daughter the stem cells was the right thing. Being here, though, in Lilac Ridge, it was all wrong, because she couldn't give Brent what he wanted, what he'd been asking for all summer.

It broke her heart, but she knew the pain she would have to survive was nothing compared to what Brent would have to endure.

After slurping the rest of her drink, she headed to the bar, climbed up on a bar stool and slid the empty glass toward Sean. "Hit me," she demanded.

"No can do, doll. I called you a ride."

"Look at me," she said, holding her hands out to show her almost perfect balance. When her body swayed to the right and she overcompensated, she decided it was best not to show off. "I can still sit upright. My instructions were,"

"It's my bar. I decide when you've had enough."

"Most of the drinks you served didn't even have tequila."

Courtney filled the seat next to her. "No more drinks," she snarled.

"Got it covered," Sean responded and sauntered off to the next demanding customer.

"What's your beef?" Tristin asked Courtney.

"You are drunk and you're shacking up at my home. Call me a bitch if you want, but I'm not holding your hair when you're praying to the porcelain god, and I'm not letting you bring my brother down too. He's been sober for years and doesn't need your drama."

"Right you are," Tristin responded. Tonight she'd be back in the camper, and tomorrow she'd be towing it to the campground, as planned. She couldn't keep shacking up with Brent, not if she expected to leave his heart intact when she left in a few weeks.

Sean moved back to them, wiping down a glass and nodding toward the door. "Your ride's here."

Tristin twisted around — much too far — and found Brent sauntering his yummy self across the pub.

She spun around to Courtney. "You ratted me out."

Courtney shook her head while Sean said, "That would be me."

She continued the spin, coming back to where she started and facing Sean. "You were supposed to call Uber?"

"I did you one better," he responded and moved to the other end of the bar.

# Chapter 11

ONE BETTER WAS right, because Brent was his own uber...uber sexy. Tristin, however, was toxic right now and didn't want to push that off onto the man she cared too much about.

His sex appeal had a direct override to her common sense, though, and maybe she was mildly intoxicated. Unable to resist his allure, she pushed off the stool and met him one, two, three steps from the bar, brushing her hands up his very fine torso and locking her fingers at the back of his neck. His mouth moved to hers with little coaxing, his arms locked, hands gripping her hips.

She wanted closer, to climb him like a tree and show Bailey how much Tristin hadn't been dumped. Brent being the sober one, kept her at an arm's length.

"You taste like tequila."

"It's ladies' night," she pointed out.

"And I heard you were a lady in need of a ride home," he said, resting his forehead on hers and touching her nose with his. Eskimo kisses, so sweet.

"I'm not done drinking."

"She's done, mate," Sean said. "These are hers."

Brent let her go and took the offering — her phone and keys.

"She settled up?"

Sean laughed. "Yeah, all set."

"I expect free drinks the next time I'm in here too," she said, pointing at him, "and not that watered-down crap you served tonight."

"You won, fair and square, but you only wagered tonight's tab."

"I said my tab. I never said tonight's tab."

Brent gave her a tug. "Come on, Tris. Let's get you home."

*Home.* That hollow feeling she'd ignored because of the buzz spread across her chest again. Tristin didn't have a home. Sure, she was shacking up with Brent, playing house, but it was only temporary. Soon she'd be on the road again, living in the camper — her home — far away from Lilac Ridge and the man she didn't deserve.

As if the two of them belonged together, Brent slid his arm around her shoulder and led her out of the pub. She caught sight of Bailey scowling at them for which Tristin mentally patted herself on the back. They rode back to Brent's in silence, at least until they hit his driveway. "You can drop me at the path to the camper."

"Why?" he grunted.

"Because that's where I live. That's home."

"You're hammered. I'm not leaving you alone."

"I won't be alone. Cyn is there."

"No, she's still at the pub."

Where Tristin should still be.

Brent drove past the path and down the driveway to his house. She got out before he came around, but he was there before she shut the door, holding out his arm and closing the door for her. When they got inside, he grabbed two Coke's from the fridge. "You need to sober up a little or you'll be nursing a hell of a hangover tomorrow."

"I didn't drink that much." Brent chuckled at her slurred words and she stuck her tongue out at him.

"According to Sean, you did."

"Rat-fink," she mumbled. If it wasn't for those watered-down drinks, she'd have some hope of having that hangover tomorrow, the only thing to keep her from feeling anything except empty.

"You want to talk about it?" he asked, taking a seat on the opposite end of the couch from where she'd settled.

"Sure don't." She crawled across the couch, stalking her prey like a wild cat. Heat flashed in his eyes, an invitation, so she went straight for his belt. His hand fell on hers.

"What are you doing?"

"Having my wicked way with you," she said.

Brent shook his head. "Not when you're hammered."

"It's not like we don't do this every night...and every morning..." she giggled, "and every afternoon."

"Doesn't matter how often we make love, Tris, we're not doing it when you drank yourself stupid and won't tell me why."

"Oh, so you're going to dangle sex in front of me to get me to air my dirty laundry."

"No. You don't have to talk but even if you do, we're not making love tonight."

"Making love isn't what I had in mind."

He just grunted and shifted, but she could see how aroused he was. He might talk a good game, but the body didn't lie. "You want me."

"I always want you."

"And you'll deny yourself because I had a few margaritas?"

He nodded this time.

Tristin hated men. This was why her relationships since Mark had been casual. This, with Brent, was supposed to be casual too. Just the summer. That's all they had, yet he wanted to throw away an entire night because she'd tossed back a few?

Fine. Whatever. If he wanted to play hardball, yeah, she could play hardball too.

Standing, she tore her shirt over her head, released her bra and shrugged out of it in about two beats. She employed less grace when trying to lose her pants. With a roll onto the floor that included a hard and loud thunk, she recovered fast enough that Brent didn't have a chance to rescue her. With a few more kicks, she freed herself from the pants and panties.

Brent's usual narrow and piercing eyes widened, his pupils dilating. She had his attention now.

~ ♥ ~

A lesser man would cave, strip down, and take her right then and there without thinking twice.

Brent was not a lesser man, but as Tristin's fingers circled her bare nipples, his resolve began to plummet.

There was only one thing to do. He bolted off the couch, scooped her into his arms and headed for the bathroom. After standing her in the shower and ensuring she wasn't going to topple over, he turned on the water. Not cold, but not all that warm either.

She laughed. "A cold shower? Seriously?"

"Cool off. Sober up. I'll make you something to eat."

He left her there, doing who knows what to herself, and headed to the kitchen. His dick was hard enough to carve a log, but he wouldn't act on it. He had a code and taking advantage of a drunk woman went against everything he believed in.

He went for fast and easy, cooking up some ground beef to go with the jar of spaghetti sauce he pulled from the cupboard.

He was hungry too, so he cooked the full box of spaghetti.

It was about twenty minutes later when the water cut off in the shower. A few minutes later, Tristin appeared in the kitchen, wearing his big t-shirt that she'd claimed after her first night in his bed.

He'd half expected her to be naked, and was only a little disappointed. Her playfulness was gone now, both a relief and heart-wrenching since sadness had settled in.

"Want to talk about it?" he asked, curious what had happened.

"No," she said, settling into a chair at the farmhouse table.

Brent didn't push because he wasn't *that* guy. He mixed the sauce and spaghetti together because he remembered that's how she liked it. She smiled when he served her. When he joined her, she just twirled the fork in the spaghetti.

"I'm not a bad person," she mumbled.

She was the sweetest, most generous person he'd ever met. How she thought she could be a bad person…

"I'm going to hurt you," she said, the utter lack of emotion in her voice and the fight in her eyes cutting right through his heart. "I'm not staying. I have three weeks left in Lilac Ridge and them I'm leaving. Wyoming first, then San Diego. Who knows where after that. I'm not a stay in one place kind of person."

He didn't believe that, not for a second. Something scared her, whatever had inspired her into a drinking fit, but once it blew over, once he proved…

There was only one thing he could do. He had to set aside his own fears, stand up and be a man.

"I love you, Tristin."

She shook her head, but the tears pooling contradicted her words. "You don't love me. You love the fantasy that's been building inside you all these years, an impossible dream."

"It's not impossible. That radio dedication, that was impossible, but you're here, you came because those feelings still existed inside you."

"I came because Cyn sabotaged our Wisconsin plan."

He knew Tristin, she was strong, independent. She wouldn't have let Cyn force her here. "There was more to it than that."

"Fine, I was curious, but it doesn't change anything. I'm not staying."

"What are you running from?" he growled, desperate to know what had scared her today.

Her hands landed on her hips first, then she crossed the over her chest. "I'm not running. I've built a life for myself, one that I love."

"A new place every few months is hardly a life. I've lived that, Tris, I know."

"Do not compare what I've built to what you suffered through."

The circumstances were different, yeah, but the result was the same. "You are running. Is it because of your daughter?"

Now her tears spilled and he felt like an ass for pushing. He never pushed, ever, because he didn't like to meddle in other people's business. If people wanted to share, they would, and if they didn't, who was he to force them?

But, this, with Tristin, he had to push because he couldn't convince her to stay if he didn't know why she was always on the move.

She pushed the plate across the table and stood, swiping at the tears. "I'm not hungry."

"Tris, don't go."

Putting up her hand, she shook her head. "I can't do this now."

"When, then? You've been here over a month and said you'd tell me what happened."

"Don't think that just because I'm a little drunk, I'm going to pour my heart out about her, because I won't."

She bolted across the kitchen and into the living room. Brent raced after her, catching her arm as she pushed open the screen door. She didn't resist as he pulled her against him, his arms wrapping around her.

Jesus, he could be an ass sometimes. It's no wonder he couldn't make any of his past relationships work. "I'm sorry," he murmured, kissing the top of her head.

"You haven't done anything wrong. It's me. I'm the one who's emotionally unavailable."

"I don't believe that for a minute." He couldn't believe it. She was the sole reason his heart beat, not for lack of emotion, but because she had enough for the both of them.

# Chapter 12

BRENT DESPISED WAKING up alone, but he wasn't surprised to find Tristin's side of the bed empty. After coaxing her to stay last night, he'd held her close until she fell asleep and rolled onto her stomach like she always did.

He slipped on jeans and headed downstairs, but there were no sounds from the kitchen, no coffee aroma. He peered out the back door, but she wasn't on the patio where she sometimes enjoyed her morning coffee.

Slipping on flip flops, he headed out the front door and up the path to her camper. When the path opened to the clearing, his heart sunk at the sight of her hooking up the RV to her truck.

"What's going on?" he asked.

She jumped a little and swore before turning to face him. "I wasn't going to leave without letting you know."

"Where are you going?"

"I booked a site at the campground. I think it's better—"

"Bullshit," he interrupted.

"Brent,"

"No, Tris, I'm not letting you run away."

"I'm not running away. I'm leaving in a few weeks, so it is better if we take a little distance now. Maybe it won't hurt so much when I head to Wyoming."

It was going to hurt like hell if she left, but Brent was determined to change her mind. First, he had to get to the bottom of what had happened yesterday.

"Come with me," he said. If he expected her to open up, he had to do the same.

"Where?" she huffed.

"Just come with me." He held out his hand and she took it. He led her down the path back to his house, crossing over the driveway and following another path into the woods.

She gasped when they reached their destination. "Your old Jeep."

"Another reminder of what I almost lost. It wasn't one time, Tris, I was a drunk, just like my parents. I should have died that night."

She squeezed his hand. "I'm glad you didn't and that no one else was hurt."

"It's not something I talk about, or even dwell on. Like I said before, I got my shit together and I've been sober ever since."

"You should be proud of that."

"I am and I wouldn't go back for anything. You say I'm serious now, but I'm struggling, Tris. It's not that I want to drink, I don't, but when I drank, everything was easy. Talking to people, laughing, it was all easier because I didn't give a shit about responsibility or what people thought of me. I could take women home and not feel bad about walking away from them the next morning or a week later or a month later."

"I'm not sure what you want me to say," she said.

"I don't want you to say anything, just listen, please."

She nodded and Brent dug deep for the courage to tell her the rest. "Being sober was hard because I thought about you, too much. When I met you, I was happy, for the first time in my life. When I sobered up, I tried to find that again. No one has ever made me feel Tristin, no one but you."

"You put me up on this pedestal I don't deserve. You shouldn't measure every woman you date against me, especially the seventeen year old me. I'm not that person anymore."

"I don't measure them against you. It's about happiness. I've only ever felt that with you. It's easy, even sober, because it's organic. I don't have to dig for it or be someone I'm not. I don't want to give that up, not again."

~ ♥ ~

Every word he spoke broke her heart because she couldn't give him what he wanted. "I was in an accident," she started, sucking in a deep breath while searching for the courage to tell him everything. She circled the mangled Jeep, brushing her hands across the rusty exterior and through the weeds that had grown through it. "It was a drunk driver. That's why I lost my daughter, in utero."

"Jesus, I'm sorry—"

She held up her hand, cutting him off. "I was just a month from graduating from college when I found out I was pregnant. Mark and I had been going out for about a year. We were pretty serious, I guess, but we both had plans that didn't match up, so I wasn't convinced we'd be able to make it work after graduation. Of course, getting pregnant changed that."

Story of her life, having different plans than the man she cared about. As much as she wanted to be with Brent when she was seventeen, she was going off to college in Seattle and he was staying in Lilac Ridge. They lived in different worlds then, just as they did now.

"Mark had a job lined up in Seattle. My parents were in

San Antonio by then, so I was going to check things out there and decide where I wanted to be. I'd been in Seattle for four years, I was ready for a change. Anyway, Mark asked me to marry him, insisted really. My parents pressured me. They're still traditionalists when it comes to that. So, I got a job at a hospital in Seattle and moved in with Mark while we planned the wedding."

Brent moved in, cupping her cheek, but she shrugged him away as the first tear drifted down her cheek.

Despite the clear blue sky beyond the trees that surrounded them, a dark shadow moved in with the memory. "At twenty-eight weeks, I was driving home from work when the accident happened. I was in a coma for three weeks. When I woke up, Angelica was gone. When I was brought in, they couldn't find a heartbeat, so they performed a Cesarean, but they couldn't save her."

"Jesus, Tris, I'm so sorry."

She tucked her arms in, trying to ward off the shivers that ravaged her body. "I never got to see her, never got to hold her. It took a long time for me to get over that."

Getting over it was such a fantasy, Tristin knew that. She'd gotten over it as best a mother could, but after yesterday's phone call, she knew she'd never truly get over losing her daughter.

"You don't have to—"

"Let me finish. I want you to know. I didn't marry Mark. He still wanted to, but I resented him after that. He got to see our baby, hold her, and I didn't. I was in Seattle because of him. If I hadn't been there, the accident never would have happened. I know now all of that wasn't fair to him, but it's the only way I could cope with it all. My parents continued to pressure me to marry him, to work through it, and I made it as far as the last pew at the back of the church. My feet froze. I couldn't go through with it. I didn't want to stay there, with him, in the city where my daughter died before she even got to live. I walked out."

"Do you still love him?" Brent asked.

Tristin shook her head. "I'm not sure I ever did. I went to Vegas, I drank and I met someone. Jesse. I was out of my mind with grief and he made me forget. Well, I'm sure all the tequila helped too. Anyway, I wanted to cling to that forever, so when he suggested we get married, I jumped right on that. I made it down the aisle that time, but when it came time to say our vows, I couldn't. I walked out. Again."

"Tequila. That's what you were drinking last night."

Tristin nodded. "Mark called me yesterday. I haven't talked to him since our wedding day."

"Why'd he call?" Brent prodded.

The tears poured now, she didn't even try to blink them back. "He's married, has a daughter."

"Son of a bitch," he growled, slamming his fist on the hood. "If he called—"

"She has leukemia. I saved Angelica's cord blood. That's why he called. His daughter needs a stem cell transplant."

"Shit, Tristin."

"I didn't even ask his daughter's name. All I could think about was my own grief. I'm a nurse and all my training and experience just…"

"You lost your daughter, of course your own grief is going to take hold."

"It's not who I am," she yelled. "I don't do self-pity. I'm not selfish, but every time I get involved with someone, I lose a piece of myself. The nurse in me jumps to help anyone, no matter what, but yesterday I hesitated, I didn't care about what Mark might be dealing with, I just got sucked back into my own grief."

"You get to mourn your daughter," he said.

"I did. It's been five years."

"I'm no expert here, but I'm pretty sure there's no end date on that kind of loss."

Maybe not, but that didn't warrant the way she'd reacted to Mark yesterday. She looked at the Jeep. "Why do you keep this?"

"Like I said, to remind me what I could have lost."

"And what is that?" she asked.

"Everything. That's why I'm not willing to let you walk away. I can't lose you again."

Tristin sighed, tugging on the last string of fight she had left in her. "I don't want to hurt you."

His hand cupped her cheek, the scrape of his rough skin an enticing and soothing invitation to lean in to his touch. "Do you love me?" he asked.

The question gutted her. "How I feel doesn't change anything, so it doesn't matter."

"It matters to me."

"It's not that simple, I…"

"It is that simple. You either love me or you don't."

She should say she didn't, spare them both the heartache, but Tristin didn't lie, not ever. If anything, she was brutally honest and he knew that. That's what he was asking her to be now.

"Yes, I love you, but,"

He put a finger over her lips to stop the string of reasons why they shouldn't love each other. "If all we have is three more weeks, I'll take it, but I think we can have so much more. Like you've been saying all summer, I don't think we should waste a moment."

# Chapter 13

IT HAD TAKEN a week to deal with all the paperwork that involved releasing Angelica's stem cells to Mark. He exercised more patience than she did, but Brent stood by her through every meltdown and tantrum she had. While it should have cut through the ice in her heart, all it did was remind her how much she was going to hurt him when she left.

They were down to their last ten days, and tonight they were baking a hundred brownies because Courtney had organized a bake sale and adoption night at the animal rescue. Tristin didn't have a stake in any of this, but she wanted to help.

Honestly, she'd be doing herself a favor if she learned to say no, but she was a sucker for a friend in need and Courtney was a friend. Tristin just hoped she would still be a friend when she left Lilac Ridge. Courtney wasn't going to take kindly to Tristin hurting Brent and the only thing Tristin would bet on right now was that leaving would cut deep.

Maybe little bit into her heart too.

Okay, a lot, but it was nothing she hadn't survived before.

"It smells like heaven in here," Cyn said as she plopped down at the table and stuck her finger in the batter.

"Do not double dip," Tristin warned.

"Nag," Cyn whined, grabbing one of the empty bowls and diving in head first.

"Hey," Brent groaned, "I was saving that."

"You snooze, you lose, big fella" Cyn responded, chocolate spattered on her nose and forehead. "Anyway, I need to talk to you. Can you put that pan in and take a walk?"

"About what?" Tristin asked. Cyn never wanted to talk privately. She wasn't one for secrets.

"About stuff."

"Go," Brent encouraged, "I can take care of the brownies."

Tristin kissed him, tasting chocolate and coffee and all man. It was so good, she went back for more.

"Talk and walk, not give me a free show," Cyn said.

She seemed a little grumpy, an unusual emotion for her happy-go-lucky friend. "Save some batter," Tristin said to Brent, "I have ideas."

"I do love your ideas."

When Cyn sighed, Tristin took her cue to leave even though she'd rather cover Brent in batter and lick it all off. When they got outside, Cyn took a seat on one of the logs Brent had carved into a bench. "I thought we were walking," Tristin said, plopping down next to her.

"I'm staying," Cyn announced.

"You made that clear when you plopped down on the bench."

"No, not on the bench, in Lilac Ridge."

"Staying?" Tristin asked, praying she didn't already know what Cyn was talking about.

"I'm sorry. I know you're not ready to settle down, and I know I said I was with you, but I love it here and I was offered a job as nurse manager at the hospital. Courtney invited me to move into Jill's farmhouse with her. All the planets have aligned. I couldn't say no."

"But you already signed a contract for Wyoming."

"Yeah, about that. I never sent mine."

Tristin had sent hers three weeks ago. Three weeks and Cyn had said hers was handled too. "What about the RV?" They'd bought it together, 50/50, a testament to their commitment to each other and the road.

"I don't care about the RV. As far as I'm concerned, I got my investment back. It's yours, but, Tristin, come on, you can't tell me you don't love it here. Don't you want to stay, see where things go with Bear?"

She knew where they would go. He'd propose, she'd say yes, and then on the day, her cold feet would kick in and she'd run. That's what she did. Tristin wasn't the marrying type. She didn't plant roots, didn't dream about the pretty house with the white picket fence and the perfect husband and children. She cared for people when no one else could, when they faced their horrors and looked to her for hope. She didn't get attached.

"I'm going to Wyoming. I signed the contract. I'm committed."

"You can cancel it. There are jobs here."

Tristin shook her head. "I won't do that."

"Why not? It's not like leaving someone at the altar. There are plenty of nurses looking for work."

Tristin bolted off the log, turning to Cyn. "I can't believe you just threw that in my face."

"I can't believe how stupid you're being. You and Bear are crazy about each other. You can't keep your hands off each other and good Lord, if a man looked at me the way he looks at you, I'd be begging him to marry me."

Once again, Tristin wanted to ask if Cyn had met someone, but she wasn't the sneak around kind of girl. She loved to kiss and tell, so since she hadn't been telling, she hadn't been kissing. In fact, this whole situation had Tristin perplexed. Yes, Cyn had mentioned staying, but that was a passing statement, nothing solid. She wasn't the type of person to take a vindictive stab at anyone, let alone a friend. "Are you mad at me because I don't want to stay?" Tristin asked.

Cyn shook her head. "I'm mad because you can't look beyond your past to see what the future holds. What you and Bear have, it's rare, Tris, don't run from it."

The same words Brent had uttered, pleaded, but Tristin couldn't stay. This was just a fleeting moment in her life, in their lives, and because it was more than she could ever ask for, she couldn't hope for it to last.

Tristin tried to take something for herself once. She'd suffered ever since.

"I've already moved in with Courtney. I've been living there for a week. You didn't notice because you've been living here with Bear, where you belong."

Tristin didn't belong, not here, not with Brent, not anywhere. "I guess that's that, then."

"I guess so." Cyn walked away, not even looking back. Tristin fell onto the bench again, Rascal coming out from the bushes and chirping. "Hey, cutie. Let me get you a snack."

She'd seen Brent feed the raccoon enough times to know he kept a stash of dog food in a latched bin against the house. She opened the latch and grabbed a handful, securing it before sitting back on the bench and holding out a morsel for Rascal.

"Is that yummy?" she asked, holding out another piece when Rascal chirped again, but this time, she grabbed Tristin's finger and held on as she seemed to chirp a story.

"Don't gang up on me too," Tristin responded. "You'll take care of our guy after I leave, won't you."

Rascal chirped, releasing Tristin's finger before taking another morsel.

The gravel crunched beneath Brent's feet, letting her know he was there. "She doesn't let anyone else feed her," he said, "I guess that makes you special."

"I'm a nurse. People and animals trust me."

"Maybe you became a nurse because of how special you are."

She wasn't sure why she became a nurse, except that her mother loved it and Tristin had always loved helping people. There was a reward in it, helping people through a trying time, seeing the hope and the smile when things took a turn for the better. Of course, it wasn't always like that, there were times when things never took that miraculous turn. Those times hurt, but it gave her balance, made her appreciate the good times, the hope she provided.

"How are the brownies?" she asked.

"Brownies are fine. I heard some of what Cyn said. I wasn't eavesdropping, things got heated and I was concerned."

"Did you know she was moving in with Courtney?" Tristin asked.

Brent shook his head. "I had no idea, but it's not a big surprise. Those two have been tight since you rolled into town."

"I can't stay," she said.

"That's not true. You can stay, you just don't want to."

"That's not true," she echoed, but didn't have anything to support her claim, nothing of substance anyway. "I made a commitment. I can't break that."

Brent pushed aside his apprehension and asked the one question he'd been afraid to all summer. "Why did you come here, Tris?"

He hadn't asked because there was the answer he wanted and the answer he expected. This was just a summer fling for her, and while he had hoped for more, deep down, he knew she would never bend.

"You're the one who dedicated that song. You wanted me to come here."

He sat on the bench next to her, his arm going around her

shoulder so she didn't feel like he was ganging up on her too. "I know, and I'm glad you did, but I want more than the summer."

Tristin let out a long sigh and shook her head. "How many times are we going to have this conversation?"

Brent chuckled, an attempt to lighten the conversation. Trying to bust through her walls never worked, but maybe inviting her to step outside was the better approach. "Until I convince you not to leave."

Rascal chirped and waved, as if she was asking Tristin to stay too.

"If there are places you want to see, we can do that, together," he offered.

With a sigh, she leaned against his shoulder. "Sounds too good to be true."

He pulled her onto his lap, kissing the woman — and himself — senseless. That little admission was a crack in her resolve, the first one he'd breached all summer. Since Brent was better at taking action than trying to find the right words, he closed in on her lips, so soft and warm against his. The tension eased from her body as he caressed and teased. When he released her mouth, her eyes opened slowly, a little sigh escaping with her next breath.

"Marry me."

She bolted off his lap, shaking her head. "I'm not, no, I, I can't do that."

Brent hadn't intended to say it, but it's what he wanted and he'd be lying if he said otherwise. It wasn't romantic, but romance wasn't his style and it wasn't Tristin's either. She was a spur of the moment kind of person and Brent had once been that way too.

"Come on, Tris, this summer has been perfect. We fit, we always have."

"We fit because we both know I'm leaving. You have this place, it's all yours, and your business and your way of doing things."

"Yeah, and you being here has made all that better. I'm a better man when I'm with you. I don't feel like my demons are going to pull me back under, I don't have to pretend to be someone I'm not."

"And you're asking me to be someone I'm not. Listen, can we just rewind, go back to that kiss and forget you ever asked that question?"

Brent shook his head. "I can't go back." There he was, using Tristin's favorite word, but whether he couldn't or wouldn't it didn't matter. Brent tried not to live in the past, and Tristin was the one thing keeping him from going forward because he didn't want to do it without her.

"We have brownies to wrap," she said. "The adoption drive starts in a couple hours and your sister will be pissed if we're late."

Brent didn't care about the brownies or the adoption drive, or hell, even making his sister mad, but Tristin had patched up the crack in her ten foot wall and once again, Brent wasn't equipped to break through it.

# Chapter 14

IT WAS RASH, she knew, but if she wasn't famous for leaving men at the altar, she was infamous for making rash decisions.

If she stayed in Lilac Ridge, she would only continue to hurt Brent and she couldn't bare another second of that.

So she was saying her good-byes, quietly, but it wasn't going so well.

"Are you leaving now because I decided to stay?" Cyn asked. The meeting room at the Hale was full, people milling about buying baked goods, talking to Jill, Cat, and Courtney about the animals in need of adoption. Brent and Darren were huddled in a corner talking about Darren's bachelor party and Clarissa was keeping Maddie far away from the brownies, her biggest weakness.

"If you're not going to Wyoming, there's no reason for me to hang around," Tristin explained.

"No reason? What about Bear?"

"It'll be easier on both of us if I go now."

"Fine, be stupid. Leave. See if I care." Cyn stomped off in

classic diva fashion, leaving Tristin to scan the room for the next person she could disappoint.

As if on cue, Maddie walked over. "You look like someone just stole your dog."

"I was just coming to find you," Tristin lied. She'd been hoping to leave without saying good-bye to her other friends. She hated long, drawn out good-byes and they'd forgive her at some point.

"Good, if you were coming to find me, let's go over here and talk. I need to keep a reasonable distance between me and the brownies. If I get too close, I'll gain ten pounds just from the smell."

"We can go outside," Tristin suggested, away from dark eyes that kept landing on her from across the room.

When they reached the front step, Maddie let out a long sigh. "I love supporting Jilly and helping wherever I can, but a bake sale violates my eighth amendment rights."

"I believe it's only considered a violation if the government is imposing cruel and unusual punishment."

"No one likes a know-it-all, Tristin," Maddie countered. "So, tell me, what's up?"

"I'm leaving in the morning, heading for Wyoming?"

"What? Already? But, what about my wedding?"

"I know. I'm sorry, but it's time for me to go."

"What happened? Did you and Bear get into a fight? I can have Darren beat him up for you."

Tristin shook her head and laughed because even though Darren was well-built, she'd put her money on Brent taking him in a fight. "No, nothing like that."

"Talk to me, girl. You know I have insight, innate and from my long hours of schooling and providing the best quality therapeutic services anyone could ask for."

Maddie was so light-hearted, with a great sense of humor, and yeah, an innate ability to draw confessions out like a well-placed needle draws blood. "I'm hurting him by staying, so I need to go before I hurt him too much more."

"Or are you trying to avoid hurting yourself?" Maddie asked, resting a comforting hand on Tristin's shoulder.

"I never had any plans to stay," Tristin reminded her.

"Yes, but a girl can always change her mind."

Not this girl. "You are going to be so focused on Darren, you won't even miss me at your wedding."

"I miss you already and for the record, I think you're making a huge mistake by leaving. You and Bear belong together."

Seemed to be the theme of the night, but it was like the theme song for the Titanic, beautiful and heart-wrenching, signaling certain doom.

"It was great seeing you again," Tristin said. "Will you let Brent know that I headed back to his place?"

Maddie gave her a long hug, and then another before she bolted back up the stairs.

Since she insisted on riding over alone, Tristin hopped on her Harley and headed back to pack things up. The open ride and fresh air always cleared her head, and the slow, winding road gave her the time to think about her decision, reinforce her resolve. This wasn't rash, it was smart. With Cyn staying behind, she'd have to deal with the logistics, make reservations, handle every aspect of every assignment. Tristin needed to get a grip on that sooner rather than later. Maybe she'd find someone in Wyoming who shared her wanderlust and would share in the travels.

Twilight had fallen by the time she reached the RV. Even though she spent most nights in Brent's bed, her clothes and everything else remained in her portable home. Her throat tightened as she climbed inside and she wondered what it was going to be like to live in there without Cyn. They'd been together for so long, Tristin couldn't imagine life on the road without her best friend.

She had a hard time imagining life without Brent, too, but she'd known all along this was just a temporary arrangement. She didn't wait until things weren't fun anymore, always moving on before the novelty wore off, excited for the next new adventure.

Wyoming seemed like a world away.

Nothing needed to be done inside the RV. Since she hadn't spent a night there all summer and Cyn had hauled all of her stuff out and secured everything else, it was ready to be hooked up to the truck and rolled out. All she needed to do was haul her mountain bike, skis, snowshoes, and rock-climbing gear in from the trailer, then load the Harley into the back of her truck, and she could hook up and go.

When she stepped out of the RV, Brent peered at her from the picnic table. "Were you even going to say good-bye or just sneak off in the middle of the night?"

"I wasn't planning to leave until tomorrow," she said. While she wanted one last night with the man she shouldn't have fallen in love with — again — it wasn't fair to ask that of him. When she was all packed up, she had intended to go tell him her plans.

"Are you leaving because I proposed?"

"I'm leaving for a lot of reasons. The longer I stay, the more I'll hurt you."

"It can't hurt anymore than it does right now."

Maybe she never should have come. From the beginning she knew it was a bad idea. Tristin told Cyn as much, but she'd gone ahead and canceled their Wisconsin reservation and made a new one in Lilac Ridge, all before Tristin could bat an eye. Tristin had even said the car accident was a bad omen, but Cyn refused to believe. Fate was pulling them to Lilac Ridge, she'd claimed, they had to go despite the obstacles.

When she'd seen Brent after they walked into Madigan's, the last ten years had ceased to exist.

But life had a way of dishing out the bad to balance out the good. She wasn't sure she could ever walk down the aisle, feared the same panic that had gripped her the last two times would take hold again. When it did, she'd hurt Brent way worse than she was now.

# Chapter 15

EACH DAY, TRISTIN took it slow, driving until her weary mind couldn't focus on the road ahead, then exploring some random attraction until she grew bored with that. Each night, she found a quiet Wal-mart parking lot and slept in the front seat of her truck. Since she was small, it offered plenty of room, but after three days, she was ready for a bed, a shower, and a long night's sleep.

When the campground she randomly selected had space, she let out a long sigh and decided to stay for two nights. She needed out of the truck because driving for the better part of three days had done nothing to clear her head.

She missed Brent. Her brain wouldn't stop thinking about him, the hurt and resignation written all over his face as she drove away.

Even if she could forget that, her chest ached so much she could barely draw breath. The only thing that had ever hurt this much was losing Angelica.

With the help of her camping neighbors, she got the RV

secured and hooked up, and was ready for a bike ride. She lucked out with this campground as it had riding trails connected to it, so she didn't even have to beat pavement to get some quality pedal time.

After unlocking the door, she climbed in, a familiar chirp and an unpleasant smell greeting her.

No, this was bad. She couldn't…"Rascal?"

The raccoon stood in the small sink, one paw waving at Tristin. "Oh, baby, no. How did you get in here?"

She was clever, that's how. The poor thing had to be starving because the camper had been purged of all food long before Tristin prepared to hit the road. She'd been staying at Brent's all summer and apparently Cyn had been living with Courtney at Jill's farmhouse.

Tristin dug out a bowl and a bottle of water from the cupboard and poured a nice serving, setting it on the table. The poor girl had to be parched and based on how she drank and splashed, she needed the water more than anything else.

"Let me find you some food," Tristin offered. The raccoon let Tristin give her a little scratch at the top of the head before she stepped out, securing the door so Rascal couldn't get out.

"This is just great," Tristin whined, stepping out to the dirt road that would lead her to the campground's convenience store. No doubt, they would have graham crackers, maybe even dog food.

Then what? She couldn't keep Rascal despite how cute and sweet she was. She also couldn't let her go in the wild. Rascal was Brent's, she belonged with him, on his property with his perfect little cabin and the tranquility the secluded home offered.

Tristin had even managed to find peace there, something she failed to find everywhere else she had gone.

Her heart kicked up, not because of the quick pace, but because it decided to chime in on her wayward thoughts. She hadn't found peace in Lilac Ridge. She'd found it with Brent.

And then she'd run, like the scared little girl she'd always been.

"Shut up," she told the voice in her head and the hum in her heart.

It had never before bothered her to leave, not a location, not a person. She was a wanderer, whether by nurture, because as an air force brat she'd moved every few years, or by nature, maybe having been born that way, she didn't know and had never questioned it. When she got pregnant, she knew those days were over. She thought she'd been ready to settle down. Even after she lost Angelica, she thought it was still time. Her heart wasn't in it though. She didn't think she was meant to be in just one place. She also didn't think she was meant to be with anyone. Tristin wasn't the type of person to get attached — ever.

Brent changed that. Her heart ached like it never had before. It was different than the devastation she felt losing Angelica, but no less potent. Being with him, well, really, being without him, made her long for things, roots, a home, love. The one time she had planned for those things, she'd lost too much. What if something horrible like that happened again?

The little store had both graham crackers and dog food, so Tristin bought both and asked about a where she could get a small pet carrier. She had but one option, to drive back to Lilac Ridge. Even though Rascal had free reign of the RV for the past few days, Tristin thought she would be safer in a carrier.

"I also need to change my reservation," she told the woman behind the register, who had checked her in. "I can only stay for one night."

Tristin couldn't ignore what needed to be done and she didn't want to give herself time to second-guess and doubt the decision. Rascal's home was with Brent.

*Your home is with him too.*

"I know," she whispered.

"I'm sorry, what was that?" the woman behind the counter asked.

"Oh, nothing, just thinking out loud," Tristin said, not wanting to admit she was responding to the voice in her heart.

With treats for Rascal, Tristin hoofed it back to her site and was once again greeted by the sweet little chirp and wave. She opened the graham crackers and broke off a piece. Rascal reached out with two paws and took the offering, nibbling away like this was the best snack she'd ever had.

Once she'd nibbled through two whole crackers, Tristin got to work cleaning up the messes Rascal had left on the floor. Thank goodness the floor was vinyl and not carpet and that the runner extending across could just be tossed out.

When Tristin was done cleaning and sat down to come up with a plan, something normally left to Cyn, she couldn't push aside the longing for the man she left behind. Rascal stood on the bench next to her, her paw up. Tristin offered another cracker, but the critter didn't take it. She did, however, take Tristin's finger, holding it in a tight grasp the way she always did with Brent.

"I miss him too," she admitted. "I was a fool to leave."

How long would it have taken Tristin to figure that out if she hadn't found the stowaway?

"Screw it," Tristin proclaimed.

There was no time like the present and she wasn't going to get a wink of sleep thinking about Brent and hoping he would forgive her and take her back…

And what the hell, maybe even still want to marry her, since she was the queen of rash decisions.

"I'm a nut-job," she told Rascal, who chirped in response.

"What do you say we head back to our man?"

Rascal flailed Tristin's finger around in agreement before releasing it, as if telling Tristin to get off her ass and high-tail it out of here.

With her neighbor's help, who clearly thought she was crazy, she got the RV unhooked from the site and hooked back up to her truck.

Entering Lilac Ridge into the map program on her phone,

she had a good thirty-six hours of driving ahead of her. She planned to drive until she couldn't anymore, but no sight-seeing on this trip. If she put in a couple long days, she might even make it back for Maddie's wedding.

~ ♥ ~

Brent was trying to be happy for his friend, trying to be the supportive best man, but all he wanted to do was grab a chainsaw and hack up some wood.

At least he didn't want to drink himself into oblivion like he had the last time Tristin left him. That was progress.

Courtney had moved out, Tristin had left town, and even Rascal had disappeared. Seemed as though he wasn't meant to have any woman in his life.

The bride was ready to throw the bouquet and Brent was ready to get away from all the marital bliss, but his duties required him to stay, so he found a quiet table in the corner and tried to enjoy his virgin margarita. Yeah, it was a girl's drink, and yeah, it was just one more form of torture since it reminded him of Tristin, but since everything reminded him of Tristin, it didn't much matter what he drank.

Courtney took a seat next to him, a glass of soda in her hand. "Not going to join the frenzy?" he asked.

"I have to finish school before I can even think about dating, so I'm sitting this one out. You should get out there for the garter."

"I'm willing to try the dating site, but I'm not putting myself out there for a bunch of crazy women at a wedding."

"Okay, I'll grant you a stay on that one. I'm holding you to the dating site though. No more of this moping around. Someone who would leave like that isn't worth your time."

There was a big ruckus where all the women were gathered but Brent didn't pay it any attention. He was more interested in his watch and trying to figure out how long he, as the best man, had to stick around this party. He shouldn't leave until Darren did. Since they'd already cut the cake and had all the official dances, he hoped the newlyweds would want to make their exit soon.

Maddie threw the bouquet and the cheers echoed throughout the ballroom. Brent caught site of a red dress and figured one of the bridesmaids had snagged the bouquet since they were all in red gowns. Then a wave of long blonde hair grabbed his attention and he looked up to find Tristin holding the bouquet and making her way across the dance floor.

"What the…" he muttered and bolted out of the chair.

"Holy shit," Courtney echoed, and it was only then that Brent knew he wasn't imagining it.

Tristin stopped to hug Maddie, because Maddie wouldn't let her pass without a hug, but Tristin kept her gaze fixed on Brent the whole time.

Lots of head nodding and smiling followed before Tristin finished her journey. Brent met her at the edge of the dance floor.

"Tris," was all he could whisper, afraid if he said anything, he'd scare her off again.

"I'm sorry for leaving. I freaked out and then I found Rascal in the RV and I knew I had to come back."

"Rascal was in your RV?" he asked.

Tristin nodded and shook her head, her mouth forming a smile as she rolled her eyes. "The little stowaway. I made it all the way to Wisconsin before I found her

"Are you back for good?" he asked, hope flickering in his chest.

She shook her head, but her smile didn't falter. "I don't want to back out of my contract, but, I've been thinking, so much so that my head hurts as much as my heart."

He knew leaving had hurt her, too. He had seen it in her eyes, but he didn't have the words to make her stay.

"What were you thinking about?" he asked, that spark

becoming a slow burn.

"I was thinking maybe you could come with me, or visit at least, and when my contract is done in a few months, I can find a job here and we can…"

The slow burn erupted, knocking the wind out of him. He struggled for breath, for words, but fear gripped his throat, not allowing him to get purchase on either.

"Brent, do you still want to marry me?" she asked.

Tristin didn't mess with people, at least not the people she liked. She'd done a good job of messing with Bailey, but that was a different ball game. "You're serious? You're not going to run again?"

She shook her head. "I don't want to run from you. I don't want to run at all, unless we are running somewhere together. I love you, Brent Daniels and I don't want to waste another minute without you."

Because actions always spoke louder than words, Brent tugged her against him, crushing the bouquet between them. "I love you."

He wiped the smile from her lips with a kiss that threatened to set the hotel to flames. Applause echoed around them, but Brent didn't care about the audience. All he cared about was the woman in his arms, the one he wanted to make his wife.

Releasing her lips, he shook his head. "I need to buy a ring, propose to you the way a man should."

She smiled back. "I don't need those formalities."

"Take this," Maddie said, holding out her garter. "No point risking this getting into the hands of someone who doesn't deserve it."

"An engagement garter?" Tristin laughed. "I love it."

"He still has to slide it up your leg, though. Every inch equals a year of happiness for me and Darren. I expect you to take it all the way, Bear."

Brent took the garter and while he wasn't a grope his woman in public kind of guy, he'd be happy to slide this thing all the way home.

# Epilogue

SHE HAD DONE it. Tristin May — Tristin Daniels, now — had walked down the aisle, said *I do*, and kissed her husband.

"I love you," she said, smiling at the man she just couldn't leave again. Brent looked delicious in worn out jeans and a t-shirt, but in a tuxedo, Tristin had no words.

"I love you, too, Tris, more than anything."

Now she got to walk back up the aisle, no longer a bride, but a wife. Her friends were all there, Cyn of course, as the maid of honor, Maddie, Clarissa, and Jill, all smiling, Cat, a little teary-eyed.

Rascal had even made an appearance during the quiet ceremony, chirping her approval and congratulations.

Courtney was not smiling. She waited for them where the party tent had been set up in Brent's front yard. "You bring him back. If you don't, I will find you and drag him back here myself."

"I promise to bring him back," Tristin assured her new sister-in-law. Brent had agreed to go to Wyoming, and insisted they take a long honeymoon when the contract was up. With all his tools packed, he planned to keep his business going on the road. He already dealt in mail order for his carvings, so knew how to handle packaging and shipping for any signs the locals might want while he was gone.

They planned to enjoy their wedding night in the honeymoon suite at the Hale, courtesy of Jill and Austin, but they'd be on the road first thing tomorrow in order to arrive in Wyoming in time for her to start work. Tristin planned to check for stowaways this time, but assured Rascal she'd be bringing their man back.

The biggest surprise of all, was her parents. She hadn't expected them to come since they'd already paid for the big wedding once and she'd bailed. They didn't know about the near-miss with Jesse, but since they hadn't approved of Brent when she was seventeen, she didn't expect them to be receptive. Her brother couldn't get leave on such short notice, but he promised to visit if she did, in fact, plant some roots.

"I'm so proud of you," her mother, Monica, said, giving Tristin a hug. "I was surprised when you told me you were coming back here, but I wasn't surprised when you said you were marrying Brent."

"Always so intuitive," Tristin laughed, hugging her mom back.

"I'm happy for you, honey," her dad, Al, added before holding out his hand to Brent.

Brent, her husband — and yeah, she couldn't even think the word without getting giddy — shook hands with his new father-in-law.

"Maybe she'll finally settle down somewhere," Al finished.

"I think I have my work cut out for me, sir," Brent responded.

Dragging her husband away before the inquisition about children started, Tristin came to a stop at a very happy Cyn, who hooked her arm and pulled her away from Brent.

"I guess it's true what they say," Cyn said with a giggle.

"I'm almost afraid to ask," Tristin said.

"This is your third trip to the altar, and you followed through. Third time must be a charm."

# Dear Reader,

The third time certainly is a charm, at least for Tristin. I hope you enjoyed this journey into love and don't forget to read all the other stories in this series! They are all fun, fast reads.

I would love it if you would write an honest review at your preferred review site and help other readers find this and other stories. There's an excerpt from the next book in the series, *The Perfect Pairing,* and links to my other books, so keep on reading!

All the best,

Susan

Continue reading for an unedited excerpt from
*The Perfect Pairing,*
the fourth book in the Superstitious Brides series.
This novella will be available in September 2016
(ebook is part of the *Romancing the Wine* collection.

# Excerpt – The Perfect Pairing

Courtney Daniels jumped out of the way as a ragged old truck in worse condition than her Beetle tore across the gravel parking lot. Stumbling onto the hood of her car, she hollered a few colorful expletives that would have made her father proud.

"Dammit," she muttered after the dust settled. She'd spent way too much money on this dress and shoes, but both boasted successful business woman and right now, that's what she needed.

Too bad she was now covered in parking lot dust.

The fake fingernail she'd repaired on the way dangled, mocking her attempt to look professional. She flung the finger out toward the truck that had nearly run her over. "Thanks a lot, jack-ass!"

Reeling the finger in, she reminded herself there were worse things than breaking a nail. The man interviewing her probably didn't care how much she spent on this stupid manicure. He was interested in her skills, not her looks. Marketing specialists didn't need perfect nails and neither did Courtney.

She checked her watch, grateful she'd arrived early enough to freshen up before meeting with her new boss — potential new boss, anyway. She needed this job more than she needed her next breath.

Clutching her tablet in one hand, she stepped off only to fall flat on her face, another string of expletives launching into the warm, late summer breeze. Courtney peered over her should to find one of the heels dangling off the bottom of the shoe. "Please don't let this be a bad omen."

She could list at least six reasons why she didn't wear high heels. Walking barefoot on burning coals would be easier than tromping around in these three-inch heels. Now, with one of them broken, she'd be walking with a very distinct limp. Maybe her potential new boss liked women with a limp and a potty mouth. She'd be a shoe-in if he also liked dust covered power dresses and scraped knees.

She kicked out of the other heel and reach into the back seat of the convertible to grab the nail repair kit she'd bought not thirty minutes ago. The glue in the kit might just be what she needed to hold her shoe together. Courtney also grabbed the roll of black duct tape, just in case. If it could keep her 1972 Beetle from falling apart, maybe it'd keep the shoe together for this interview.

"I better get this job," she prayed while every shard of gravel cut into her foot like broken glass. The Black Vines Winery perched atop a hill, the gravel parking lot giving way to wide granite steps that elevated the building like a palace. "Guess I'll be getting my steps in today." Painful as that might be.

Growing up practically a hobbit, Courtney neither wanted nor needed shoes, but because being a grown-up bit in so many ways, her feet had gotten used to being covered. "I do not miss my combat boots," she muttered. "I do not."

After what felt like a ten-mile ruck march, she reached the flat stone walkway. The cool slate soothed her tortured feet. She stopped at the bottom of the granite steps to take in the beauty. Courtney had done her research, knew these steps had been procured from the old wooden schoolhouse when it was torn down twelve years ago. They rose like the steps of Olympus, creating a path to glory and the achievement of dreams.

Her feet enjoyed the cold granite even more than the slate as she made the climb. Between the trek across the parking lot and the climb up the steps, she should be able to lose ten pounds in no time working here. So long as the jack ass in the black truck didn't kill her.

Of course, she needed to get hired first. "Don't get cocky," she preached. Her resume didn't suck, but it wasn't all that impressive either. Courtney clung to a desperate hope that her time in the air force mattered and that maybe the hours volunteering at the animal rescue and the time she'd put in working the social media aspect of her brother's business were enough to impress Mr. Black. The fact she was twelve credits from a bachelor's degree in marketing couldn't hurt either.

And hey, this was her second interview at the winery, so obviously she'd made an impression the first time around.

The air conditioning was a slap in the face when Courtney pulled the door open. She hoped to make it to the bathroom without anyone noticing her bare feet. She scanned the large reception area, but not a soul appeared to be around. Odd, this was an upscale winery which served lunch Thursday to Sunday. Since it was approaching eleven in the morning, the place should be buzzing.

The restrooms were beyond the reception desk. As Courtney padded across the black granite floor, the phone behind the desk started ringing. Not a body stirred. No one came out of the bathroom, nor did anyone rush out of the restaurant. She should ignore it, keep walking straight to the bathroom and get herself cleaned up for the interview, but a ringing phone was like fingernails on a chalkboard. Courtney couldn't tolerate it, not for one more ring. She did an abrupt right face and marched around the desk, answering the phone like she already worked there.

"Good Morning, Black Vines Winery, how may I help you today?"

"Where's Aiden?" the woman demanded.

Courtney's interview was with one Aiden Black, who just a few months ago had inherited the winery, according to the research she'd done.

"I'm sorry, Mr. Black isn't available at the moment. Would you like to leave a message?"

"Ugh," the woman groaned. "Just tell him I got a contract and it's big money. If he wants my help, he should answer his phone. I can tell when he ignores my calls."

Courtney was about to ask exactly who was calling when silence greeted her. She made note of the message on a yellow sticky note.

"What the hell are you doing back there?" a deep voice echoed in the empty foyer. Courtney looked up to find a man with broad shoulders and an angry scowl looming over the reception desk, his dark eyes burning right through her soul.

What was she doing there? Courtney tried to remember, but the way he looked at her, angry yes, but something else too, it made her all fluttery.

"I asked what you're doing behind the desk," he said again, his voice even more demanding.

"I, you, I'm..." She paused and sucked in a deep breath, focusing on his neck instead of those penetrating eyes. Then he swallowed, his Adam's apple bobbing beneath the line where his beard ended and Courtney lost the train of thought she hadn't quite grasped again.

Shaking it off, she focused on his forehead, a technique she learned in a public speaking class. Instead of reaching across the reception desk and smoothing the crease, she licked her lips and focused on answering the question. "The phone, it kept ringing, and, well, no one was here to answer it, so I—" she extended her hand, the yellow sticky note gripped between her fingers. "This message is for you, I think, if you're Mr. Black, that is. If not, I guess you know who Mr. Black is." *Shut up, Courtney.* "She didn't leave a name."

The man dropped his chin, relenting just enough for Courtney to take a breath. She'd always thought her brother had the most intimidating scowl on the planet, but this man, wow, he made Brent look like a bear cub.

As the man read the note, Courtney eased out from behind the desk, hoping to hit the bathroom to clean up and wrestle with her bearings before she met Mr. Black. First impressions were so important and she prayed this man was just an employee and not the owner.

"Hold it," he commanded with more authority than any of the commanding officers she'd served under during four years in the air force. "What are you doing here? We're closed."

Courtney stood at attention as if commanded, her shoulders

back and her chin up, doing an about face and breathing through her nose so she could speak like a professional instead of the idiot who'd stammered her way through the previous response. "I'm here for a job interview. I'm Courtney Daniels."

"Job interview? With who?" he asked.

"With Mr. Black, sir, at eleven."

He shook his head. "With me?"

*Great. Way to make a first impression, Court. Kiss this job good-bye.*

His brow creased even further. "Son of a bitch. Who called you?"

"Amber," Courtney said, mentally checking her posture and forcing herself to breathe. "She interviewed me a couple weeks ago. She called Monday and said you requested a second interview."

"I'm gonna kill her," he muttered.

Courtney remained at attention, her bare feet rooted to the granite floor. The cold had started to seep into her body, sending a chill across her skin and up her spine.

Or, maybe that was the man. He was fierce, but she still fought the urge to touch him, to soothe the tension and…

No, no awry thoughts about the man who could be her boss. That kind of thinking led to bad decisions that would ultimately get her into trouble.

"Looks like you've been rolling in the dirt," he said, his gaze going down and back up, raising every hair on Courtney's body. "Is that how you always dress for an interview?"

"No, sir," she responded, her temper flaring as she remembered the incident in the parking lot. "I was almost rundown in the parking lot by some jack-ass in an old Ford. I got the license plate if you want to speak with whatever employee was driving like a maniac."

The bark of laughter echoed but Courtney didn't see the humor. Maybe she shouldn't have said jack ass, but sometimes her tongue had a mind of its own. It had gotten her into trouble more than once and not just while in the air force. The back of her father's hand liked to smack the smart ass right out of her when he'd had too much to drink, which was always.

"I was just on my way to the restroom to clean up before the interview."

"Interview, right," he drawled, his posture loosening. "You can forget about the interview."

"No, wait," she pleaded. "Just give me a chance. I have a copy of my resume right here." Courtney reached inside the case holding her iPad, dust flying when she pulled a paper out. "I don't have extensive experience, but the experience I do have has prepared for me a job like this. I have a lot of energy and ideas. You won't be disappointed."

"You misunderstood. You can forget the interview because you're hired. You start right now."

~♥~

# Meet the Author

Big dreamer and certifiable overachiever Susan Ann Wall embraces life at full speed and volume. She's a beer and tea snob, can be bribed with dark chocolate, and the #1 thing on her bucket list is to be the center of a Bon Jovi flash mob.

Susan is a multi-genre author of racy, rule-breaking romance, women's fiction, and erotic fiction (her erotic titles are published as Ann Victor). Her bragging rights include over a dozen books in six different series, three perfect children, two amazing rescue dogs, and a happily ever after that started while serving in the U.S. Army and has spanned two decades (which is crazy since she's not a day over 29).

In her next life, Susan plans to be a 5 foot 10, size 8 rock star married to a chiropractor and will not be terrified of large bridges, spiders, or quiet people (shiver).

Photo by BLC Photography

You can find Susan online at:
www.susanannwall.com
Facebook: Author Susan Ann Wall
Twitter: @susanannwall

# Also Available

### Fighting Back for Love Series

Relay For Love (May 2011)
A Flame Burns Inside (January 2012)
Worth the Fight (Coming Soon)

### Puget Sound ~ Alive With Love Series

The Sound of Consequence (April 2013)
The Sound of Betrayal (August 2013)
The Sound of Suspicion (January 2014)
The Sound of Deception (June 2014)
The Sound of Circumstance (December 2015)
The Sound of Reluctance (Coming Soon)

### Superstitious Brides Series

Marrying for Love (January 2016)
For the Love of Chocolate (February 2016)
3rd Trip to the Altar (August 2016)
The Perfect Pairing (September 2016)
Taking Back Good-bye (October 2016)
Mistletoe Marathon (November 2016)

### Devon Taggart Suspense Series

Broken Strings (April 2016)

### Sunset Valley Women's Fiction Series

Whisper to a Scream (May 2016)

# Multi-Author Anthologies (ebook only)

Book Boyfriends Cafe *Summer Lovin'* (May 2015)
14 summer romances from USA Today and National Bestselling
authors (includes Relay For Love)

Book Boyfriends Cafe *Tall, Dark, & Loaded* (January 2016)
6 billionaire romances from USA Today and National Bestselling
authors (includes Marrying for Love)

*Love Notes* (April 2016)
8 Country Music themed romance novels from USA Today and
National Bestselling authors (includes Broken Strings)

*Summer Solstice* (June 2016)
10 friends to lovers romances from USA Today and National
Bestselling authors (includes The Sound of Deception)

*Romancing the Wine* (September 2016)
10 wine-themed romances from USA Today and National
Bestselling authors (includes The Perfect Pairing)

*Spicy Christmas Kisses 2* (November 2016)
10 holiday romances from USA Today and National Bestselling
authors (includes Mistletoe Marathon)

www.ingramcontent.com/pod-product-compliance
Lightning Source LLC
Chambersburg PA
CBHW071259130626
46556CB00003B/1387